resolution

j. s. cooper

GALLERY BOOKS

New York   London   Toronto   Sydney   New Delhi

G

Gallery Books
An Imprint of Simon & Schuster, Inc.
1230 Avenue of the Americas
New York, NY 10020

Copyright © 2015 by Jaimie Mancham-Case

First Gallery Books trade paperback edition December 2015

GALLERY BOOKS and colophon are registered trademarks of Simon & Schuster, Inc.

For information about special discounts for bulk purchases, please contact Simon & Schuster Special Sales at 1-866-506-1949 or business@simonandschuster.com.

The Simon & Schuster Speakers Bureau can bring authors to your live event. For more information or to book an event, contact the Simon & Schuster Speakers Bureau at 1-866-248-3049 or visit our website at www.simonspeakers.com.

Manufactured in the United States of America

10 9 8 7 6 5 4 3 2 1

Library of Congress Cataloging-in-Publication Data

Cooper, J. S. (Jaimie Suzi)
Resolution / J.S. Cooper.—First Gallery Books trade paperback edition.
pages ; cm.—(Swept away ; 3)
1. Castaways—Fiction. 2. Man-woman relationships—Fiction. I. Title.
PS3603.O582637R47 2015
813'.6—dc23   2015017958

ISBN 978-1-4767-9100-5
ISBN 978-1-4767-9105-0 (ebook)

To Grandma Flo and Granddad Fred,
may you always be with me!

acknowledgments

The Swept Away series is full of mystery, intrigue, sex, and romance, and somehow it all makes sense. That wouldn't have been possible without the guidance and help of my wonderful editor, Abby Zidle; my diligent agent, Rebecca Friedman; and my great friends and beta readers, Katrina Jaekley, Tanya Kay Skaggs, Stacy Hahn, Cilicia Ann Sturgill-White, Kathy Shreve, Tianna Croy, Kanae Eddings, and Carla Short. Also, a huge thanks to all the bloggers, readers, and street team members who have supported this series. It really does mean the world to me.

prologue

"Hush little baby, don't say a fucking word," he sang in an ominous voice, twisting the lyrics to the old nursery rhyme. His voice was the only sound in the small damp space aside from a low rattling in the corner; I didn't want to know what or who was making that noise.

I kept my expression blank and my eyes downward as I sat there uncomfortably. The room was cold and dark and smelled of mold. I coughed as the mildew filled my lungs, and my body shivered on the old rickety chair I was tied to. I didn't even bother trying to scream; no one would hear me. No one would be coming to my rescue now. It was just the two of us. After everything, it had come to this. My head dropped forward with fatigue. I just wanted to sleep, but I didn't want to close my eyes. I didn't want to give him the opportunity to do something when I wasn't watching. My heart ached for the situation we were in. And I was scared. Really and truly scared, possibly more scared than I'd ever been in my life. This was different from the unknown of the island—the island had been bright and sunny, while this room was dark and dreary. This room screamed of danger, and every nerve in my body was on edge waiting to see what would happen next.

"I didn't want everything to go like this." He held the gun to my head. "You understand that, right? I didn't want to hurt you. I didn't want it to come to this."

I nodded my understanding, my throat too constricted to speak. My body was frozen in fear as an image of a black stallion running down a white sandy beach flashed into my mind. A strong, beautiful stallion with mesmerizing blue eyes. The beach reminded me of our island and the stallion reminded me of Jakob: strong, powerful, and wild. Somehow the image made me smile and calmed my nerves for a few seconds.

"A life for a life, right?" His voice sounded broken and raw. "That's what they say, right?" His voice echoed his sorrow. He didn't want to do this, but I knew he thought he had no other option. I couldn't allow myself to look up at him. All I could think was, *Is this how it's all going to end for me? Is this how my story's going to end?*

"He shouldn't have done that to my parents, Bianca." His voice was pained. "He ruined my life."

"I understand," I said softly, my voice cracking as I spoke.

I did understand. I didn't know if I could blame him. "It's not your fault."

"You're making this hard for me, Bianca." He sighed and kneeled next to me, moving the gun away from my head. He grabbed my chin and forced me to look at him. His eyes bored into mine, and I could see the regret shining at me. Regret and another emotion I recognized. My heart thudded as I stared back at him. I still had a shot at changing my story. The emotion in his eyes was one I knew well—adoration. He had feelings for me. That was the opening I needed to try to change his mind.

"You don't have to do this," I said softly. "You don't have to go through with it."

"I do," he said, but his voice was unsure as he gazed at me, his eyes scrutinizing my face.

"No. If you do, we can't be together." I nearly choked on the words, but I knew I had to say them. It was my only chance.

"You would want to be with me?" He froze. "After all this?"

"Yes." I nodded and made myself smile. "We're meant to be together, don't you see that?"

"It was always you, you know." His fingers touched my leg. "From the first time I saw you, I knew."

"So then don't do this," I pleaded with him. "This doesn't have to be the end for us. This can be the beginning."

"A new beginning?" He spoke softly, his eyes glazing over as he considered what I'd said.

"Maybe this is why everything happened," I said, my voice shaky. "Maybe we're meant to be together. Maybe this was fate's cruel joke on us. Maybe this was the only way."

"Maybe." He nodded and stepped back. My body was trembling as I waited for him to decide what he was going to do next. "You really think we're soul mates?" He stared at my lips, and it took everything in me not to shudder at his gaze. And then suddenly there was a loud bang. I screamed. He fell forward, his head hitting my lap hard, and I screamed again.

"No!" Tears fell from my eyes as a pool of red blood filled my lap. "No!" I screamed, and looked into his face. What had just happened? I wasn't even sure. Had he shot himself? He gazed at me with a weak smile, the life draining from his face.

"Your father did this to us," he mumbled. "He did this to me."

"No," I whispered, my stomach churning as I felt a wave of arctic coldness fill me. "I'm sorry," I said honestly. This wasn't how it was supposed to end.

"Hush, my little baby, don't say a fucking word," he said again, though this time his voice was but a whisper in the coldness. "This is how it should be."

"No!" I screamed this time, my voice no longer restrained by fear. I stared at his body and at the gun on the ground, just inches from my feet, the red of his blood trickling into a pool beside it.

"Please don't die," I whimpered, feeling woozy as I took a deep breath. "You didn't have to do this." Then I froze. The rattling in the corner of the room was back.

The fact that I still had company didn't make me feel better.

part 1

one

Nicholas London
Decades Ago

"Jeremiah, Larry, this is Oliver." I nodded at my new friend to enter the room. Oliver looked uncomfortable as he walked into Jeremiah's apartment. His thin frame looked particularly scrawny today, and the timid look on his face showed that he was out of his depth. Not that it mattered to me. I looked at Oliver as a kindred spirit. We were both outsiders at Harvard University, both of us having grown up in lower-class families and neighborhoods. Neither one of us was accustomed to the wealth of someone like Jeremiah Bradley. I'd been shocked when Jeremiah had approached me during freshman year and asked if I wanted to be a part of his English study group. Not that I'd known then what being a Bradley really meant, but I knew from his crisp white Oxford shirt, khaki pants, and Docksiders that he was a step up from my Bushwick roots. He'd had a self-assured grin on his face, his perfectly even, shining white teeth beaming at me as he waited for the answer he knew was coming. His golden-blond hair hung casually in his face, and his bright blue eyes glittered as he'd told me that he had his own apartment, so it would make studying easier. I hadn't known how to respond. I'd been so impressed that he could afford to own a Boston apartment.

"Hello, Oliver." Jeremiah looked Oliver up and down with an imperious stare. I noticed that he'd lost the open, engaging expression he had when we were freshmen. I could still remember the day he'd welcomed me with a huge grin. It saddened me to see how much he'd changed in such a short span of time—though a part of me wondered if he'd changed, or if he was simply revealing his true colors.

"Hello. It's nice to meet you." Oliver extended his right hand to shake Jeremiah's, and Jeremiah laughed.

"This isn't a business deal. We don't need to shake hands."

"Sorry." Oliver looked down, and I frowned. Did he have to be so shy and submissive? "My sister always told me to shake hands when I met new people."

"What's your name?" Larry jumped up from the couch and walked over to Oliver. Peering into Oliver's face, he looked at me and raised an eyebrow as if to say, *Who is this?* Larry Maxwell was Jeremiah's best friend. They had gone to boarding school together, and while Larry was also from a more modest background, he gave off a similar air of privilege.

"Oliver."

"Oliver what?" Larry rolled his eyes. All that mattered to Larry was status. Sometimes I wondered if he was friends with Jeremiah because he liked him or because of who his parents were.

"Oliver Case." Oliver looked confused, and I felt slightly sorry for him. Maybe I shouldn't have brought him over. Maybe Oliver wasn't right for our group. Maybe I should have just left him sitting alone in the chemistry lab we shared and just pretended that I didn't notice how lonely he looked. Though, I knew I couldn't have just left him there week after week. Not when he reminded me so much of myself. Not when I knew what it was like to be the odd man out. Plus, I liked him. Not just because he was poor like me, but because he was smart. He was interested in science and being innovative. He was interested in creating, and that was my life. It was also something Larry and Jeremiah cared nothing about. Larry wanted to go to law school, and Jeremiah was going to take over his family business. They were just at Harvard because it was expected of them. They weren't here for the academics. Not like me and Oliver. We were both here on scholarships, and we both enjoyed the rigorous academic standards to which we were held.

"Case, as in the Cases from the Midwest?" Larry looked impressed. "The tractor people?"

"No." Oliver laughed out loud. "The Cases from Maryland, by way of several Eastern European countries."

"Your last name isn't Eastern European," Larry said with a frown.

"My mother married an Englishman," Oliver stated simply.

"So your dad is English, then?" Larry continued his questioning as if he were already a lawyer.

"No." Oliver shook his head. "I don't have a dad."

"He died?" Larry looked surprised, and even Jeremiah looked curious.

"No," Oliver said again, without explaining further. I could see from Larry's face that he was getting frustrated, so I changed the subject.

"Oliver is in some of my science classes, and we're in the same chemistry lab. He's working on a self-painter."

"Self-painter?" Larry scoffed. "As if." He turned to Jeremiah and yawned. "Do you want to go and get milk shakes? We can see if Angelina and Brigitta are available."

My heart thudded as he mentioned Angelina Walker. Angelina Walker was the prettiest girl at Harvard—at least I thought so. She was beautiful and intelligent and sweet . . . and she was also dating Jeremiah. That meant she was off-limits to me, which was one of the hardest parts of my life, because I believed myself to be in love with Angelina Walker. Unfortunately for me, she only seemed to have eyes for Jeremiah.

"Maybe later." Jeremiah dismissed Larry, and looked at Oliver with more interest. "So what's this self-painter you're talking about, then?"

"It's a machine that will be able to paint a room in minutes, without leaving splotches or white spots," Oliver said simply. "It also contains a primer, so it will look as if a professional has painted several coats of paint."

"Wow, a machine can do that?" Jeremiah said, impressed.

"Well, I'm still working on the prototype," Oliver said excitedly. He completely changed when he talked about science and his inventions—he stood straighter, his voice no longer shook, and suddenly you couldn't help but listen to him. "But yes, I think it will work." He looked pleased with himself. "It will completely revolutionize the painting industry."

"What size room will the machine be able to paint?" Jeremiah said casually, his eyes glued to Oliver.

"I'll have different machines." Oliver shrugged. "So basically, I should be able to paint any size room in minutes, with the right equipment."

"That would be amazing for construction and contractors." Jeremiah nodded.

"I guess." Oliver shrugged. "I haven't thought that far."

"Well, that's why I'm here." Jeremiah smiled. "It helps to have friends with business minds."

"I don't have any friends with . . . ," Oliver started, and then stopped as he looked at Jeremiah's grinning face. "I guess not until now."

"Not until now." Jeremiah grinned and then put his left arm around my shoulder and his right arm around Oliver's shoulder. "Now you have us." He laughed. "Thanks to Nick for introducing us. Now we can be the Musketeers."

"There are only three musketeers," Larry said with a sour face.

"Well, there are four of us now," Jeremiah said sharply, and gave Larry a look.

"Well, there should be only three." Larry walked toward the kitchen. "I'm going to get a beer."

"We'll all have one," Jeremiah stated, and followed Larry. "We need to celebrate our new friendship." He nodded to himself as we walked, and I heard him mumbling something about "million-dollar ideas." As I stared at Oliver, looking pleased and anxious at the same time, I wondered if I had made a mistake bringing him here. I studied how his eyes widened as we walked into the opulent kitchen, with the Carrera marble counters, stainless steel appliances, and hanging copper pots and pans. The kitchen belonged in a *Better Homes* magazine, not in the apartment of a college junior who never studied—or cooked.

"Bud Light okay?" Jeremiah handed a can of beer to Oliver.

"It's great, thanks," Oliver said, nodding enthusiastically, and it struck me that this might be the first beer he'd ever had. "Thanks." He turned to me and gave me a small smile. "I'm glad we're friends, Nicholas. Thank you for introducing me."

"You're welcome." I smiled, though I still wasn't sure I'd made the right decision.

"And if the offer still stands, I'd be happy for you to help with the self-painter," he said magnanimously. "I want to test the cohesive bonds of some of the chemicals I'm using, so maybe we can go in the lab tomorrow and work on them."

"Sounds good." I nodded, and I saw Jeremiah staring at me with a determined look. I wasn't sure what he was thinking, but the uneasy feeling that filled me was getting a little too familiar.

two

Bianca London
Present Day

"Wake up, Bianca." His voice was rough as he shook my shoulder, and I opened my eyes slowly as I sat up.

"Ouch." I rubbed my head where it had hit the floor and tried to stand.

"You fainted," he said stiffly as he offered me a hand to help me up. I ignored his hand and glared at him.

"What are you doing here, Steve? Are you following me?" I snapped at him, anger overtaking any fear that I had at his presence.

"Really, Bianca? That's what you're asking me?" He looked annoyed, and I stared at his thin face in distaste. What was Steve doing here? And why was he texting me and following me around? I hadn't seen him since I'd been on the deserted island with him and Jakob, and we hadn't exactly ended our time there with kisses and hugs. "I'd have thought you'd be a bit more—"

"Enough, Steve." Rosie's voice appeared to come from out of thin air, but then I peered behind Steve and saw my best friend standing in the shadows. A best friend whom I didn't know at all, apparently.

"Rosie," I said stiffly as I stared at her face, so familiar and yet so distant. "I thought it was you I saw."

"You fainted on us." She didn't smile as she walked closer, and my head started pounding. I moved toward her, and she held her hand up.

"Stop." She shook her head. "Don't move any closer."

"Rosie." My voice cracked as I gazed at her. "Why are you doing this?" As I stared at her, I couldn't help but wish that Jakob were here with me, holding my hand, providing me comfort and poignant, loving glances to keep me strong.

She looked away from me then, her eyes leaving mine in a sort of shame.

"Rosie, please, let's talk," I called out to her, but she turned her back on me.

"So, Bianca, was your only question to me am I following you?" Steve asked with a wide smile. I could tell he was enjoying the tension in the air and the sense of powerlessness I was feeling.

"No, the question I want to ask you is if you were working for Jakob or David or Larry or someone else. And if you

were working with Jakob, why did you disappear? And exactly
what do you know about the kidnapping? And what exactly is
your role in all of this?" I spoke to him, but Rosie was the one
I really wanted answers from.

"That's a lot of questions." His thin lips attempted a
smile. "Questions I don't have to answer. What did your boyfriend, Jakob, have to say to all these questions?"

"Obviously, I don't know Jakob as well as I thought I
did," I muttered, staring at the TV screen in front of me.
The screen was now blank, but I remembered seeing Jakob
and David on it just a few minutes ago. What had David
been talking about? What had Jakob planned, and what
was he still trying to do? Though I didn't know what exactly was going on—and a part of me still struggled to trust
Jakob fully—I knew instinctively there was more than met
the eye.

My head was spinning; I needed to speak to Jakob. Not
only to make sure he was okay, but also to get as many facts
as I could that might help me understand what was going
on. After all of our back-and-forth, I had finally started to
trust Jakob. Yes, there were still doubts in my mind—I mean,
what kind of fool would I have to be if I just blindly trusted
the man who had staged our kidnapping to a deserted island
and then pretended to be someone else? Well, he'd been himself, but he hadn't told me that he was also the son of the
man I believed responsible for my mother's death. A man my
mother might also have had an affair with. A man who had
ruined so many lives.

"What are you thinking about?" Steve's eyes narrowed as he surveyed my face. And I could see Rosie looking at me from out of the corner of her eye.

"I'm thinking about how confusing this all is, and I'm thinking about Jeremiah Bradley." I sighed. "I want to know what Jeremiah Bradley was like and who he was and how he could have caused so much damage in so many people's lives."

"He was the devil." Steve looked away from me then, his mind somewhere else. "He was the devil, and one day he will burn in hell."

"I thought he was your mentor," I said, surprised at the hatred and vehemence in his voice. "I thought you loved him."

"Well, you thought wrong." He looked at me, and his eyes softened as he took in my appearance. "You look very beautiful today."

"Thank you." I didn't know what else to say, though I wasn't that grateful for him noticing my appearance. Rosie turned toward us then, her eyes narrowing as she looked at Steve. I realized then that she was wary of him; suspicious, even. Perhaps they weren't quite the united front I had thought them to be.

"Just think, if things had been different, we might have been together." Steve took a step toward me, and Rosie took a step toward him. I knew she wasn't concerned for me. She was more concerned that somehow I'd be able to flip a switch in his head and get Steve on my side. I looked at Rosie then, a deep, questioning look. A look that told her of how heart-broken I was by her betrayal—but she didn't even flinch. I stifled a sigh and looked back at Steve.

"I think that was never going to be a possibility," I couldn't stop myself from responding as my body gave an involuntary shudder. Hell no. There was no way I would ever sleep with someone like Steve. I had absolutely no attraction to him. None at all.

"What's wrong with me?" His shoulders hunched. "Am I not good enough for you?"

"What are you talking about?" I said with a frown as his expression changed. I was aggravated, and I knew I was making the situation worse. "There's nothing wrong with you," I said, trying to smile and soften my voice. "It was just bad timing for us, Steve." I choked the lies out, but I knew my best defense would be to butter him up.

"I'm always being rejected," he said, almost under his breath. I could see a flash of something looking like pain in his eyes. For a split second I felt sorry for him, but then I remembered the situation I was in. If I was going to feel sorry for someone, I knew that I was the only recipient I needed to care about.

"I think you're a good guy, Steve," I said, almost pleading as I tried to make eye contact with him. I needed to create a connection with him. I needed him to trust me.

"That's funny. Rosie seems to think you don't trust me," he said bitterly. I watched as Rosie smiled slightly and rubbed his shoulder, and I wondered what she'd been telling him. She whispered something into his ear, and his expression turned cold.

"What would you ask Jeremiah Bradley if you could talk to him now?"

"What does it matter?" I said, annoyed. "It's not like I can ask him."

"You know what I'd ask him?" Steve said softly, his voice tinged with venom.

"What?" I said, my voice barely louder than a whisper.

"I'd ask him *why*." He looked into my eyes. "I'd ask him why he had to target my dad. Why he had to ruin my life. Why he had to be so greedy." He clenched his fists. "But maybe I'll be able to get my answers one day."

"What do you mean?" My heart thudded.

"Maybe I'll be able to figure out why Jeremiah Bradley ruined my father's life," Steve said, and walked to the front door, Rosie by his side.

"How?" I followed behind him, not sure why I didn't just let him leave.

"Maybe the answers didn't die with him." He turned back and looked at me. "Maybe there is life after death after all."

"What are you saying?" I gasped, my face turning white as I tried to understand him. Was he saying that Jeremiah Bradley was still alive? Was he the mastermind behind my kidnapping?

"I'm saying that this doesn't start or end with your mother's death, Bianca." His eyes pierced mine, and the cold apathy in his gaze stung my very core.

"Where *does* it start and end, then?" I asked, my voice a mere whisper as he took a step toward me. I looked over at Rosie, and a little whimper escaped my throat. "Why are you doing this, Rosie? What have I ever done to you?"

"You would never understand, Bianca." She shook her head.

"You were my best friend. . . ." My voice trailed off. "I just don't understand. Is this because of my dad dying? Is this because of David? Are you upset that I kissed him? Is that how all this started?" I pretended to be completely ignorant—I wasn't about to reveal that I knew she was Larry's daughter, at least not yet. I was going to keep all my cards to myself until she let something slip.

"It starts with my father," Steve spoke up, and his voice cracked. "It starts with a poor, young, brilliant student at Harvard University by the name of Oliver Case."

"And where does it end?" I didn't want to tell him that I didn't know who Oliver Case was, because that wasn't exactly true. I vaguely recalled my father telling me about an old friend of his—an old friend called Oliver.

"It ends with the destruction of the Bradley brothers." Steve gave me a half smile. "And the destruction of everyone else that led to my father's death."

I swallowed hard as I stared at him, the ringing in my ears

becoming louder as my heart thudded. Who else had been re-sponsible for his father's death? How had his father died? And most important of all, was I on his hit list?

"Where are you going?" I said after a few seconds of the three us just standing there. "You're going to just leave me?"

"What did you think we were going to do?" Steve blinked at me, his face a blank slate and his eyes impassive.

"I thought you were going to take me with you." I bit my lower lip. "I thought you were going to kidnap me again."

"I didn't kidnap you in the first place. Neither did Rosie." He shrugged. "We just wanted to make sure you were watching the TV screen."

"Why?"

"I wanted to make sure you saw the sort of men you were consorting with."

"I'm not consorting with anyone."

"You shouldn't be with either of the Bradley brothers."

"Jakob is a good guy," I said weakly.

"Even you don't believe that." He laughed bitterly as Rosie snorted.

"He is." My voice was more assertive, even though I didn't feel that confident inside.

"Yeah, keep telling yourself that." He gave me a disdainful look. "I'm not going to waste my time trying to warn you to stay away from him anymore. You can make your own stupid mistakes."

"What do you care?"

"Your mother realized her mistake." Steve smirked. "Maybe you should realize yours before it's too late."

"What are you talking about?" My heart pounded as I gazed at him. Was he confirming that my mother had had an affair with Jakob's dad? Had my mother really been Jeremiah's mistress?

"You don't know?" He laughed, his eyes crinkling in a bitter way as he surveyed my face. "This all started because of her." Rosie looked at me in disgust.

"My mother had an affair with Jeremiah? So it's true, then?" I gasped, my hand flying to my mouth as despair filled my heart. My mother wasn't the woman I had thought she'd been. My heart broke for my father and the pain he must have experienced. How heartbreaking that must have been for him.

"I'm shocked you don't know about the Angelina, Nicholas, and Jeremiah love triangle." Steve looked at me in pity. "Wars have been fought for less."

"I . . ." My voice trailed off as I stared at him. I didn't even know what to say. I wasn't sure how much heartbreak I could take in one day.

"Isn't it funny how love can turn the heads of even the most brilliant and powerful men?" Steve grabbed a small flask out of his pocket and took a swig. He chugged greedily, and I watched as a trickle of brown liquid streamed down the side of his lips and to his chin. He wiped it away with the back of his hand and then licked the liquid off of his skin, slurping it up. I tried not to shiver as he flicked his tongue at me perversely and then started drinking again. The room was quiet as he stood there, just staring at me. He took another gulp of the golden-brown liquid before speaking again. "Women can ruin everything. Absolutely everything."

three

Nicholas London

Decades Ago

The music was booming by the time I made it to Jeremiah's apartment. The lights were off, and the living room was filled with a myriad of people dancing, drinking, and laughing. I looked around to see if I could spot any of my friends. I wasn't really one for partying, but I'd still come. Jeremiah expected his closest friends to attend his many events, and I was grateful to be in that circle. And I was also interested in seeing Angelina. I loved spending time with her, even though it was usually in the presence of Jeremiah. I wasn't sure what she saw in him, or why she dated him.

For that matter, I wasn't sure what Jeremiah saw in her. She wasn't his type; she seemed too quiet and shy for him. I half wondered if he was still dating her because she was the only girl who hadn't slept with him yet. She was a challenge to Jeremiah, and he liked that. It was probably part of why I was so interested in her too. Okay, more than interested. I felt a connection with Angelina that I had never felt with anyone else. It was weird because we'd never kissed, never even really touched; yet I felt connected to her in a way that made my heart leap whenever I saw her.

"Nicholas, you made it," a soft voice said in my ear, and I looked around and saw Angelina's sweet smile.

"Hey." I smiled at her and watched as she played with her long brown hair.

"I wasn't sure you were going to come," she continued, and her hazel eyes looked uncertain.

"I can't miss a party of Jeremiah's," I said softly, and she nodded.

"True, you can't do that." She moved closer to me. "So how are you? I haven't seen you in a while."

"I've been busy in the lab." I nodded and spoke into her ear, so she could hear me over the increasingly loud music. "I'm helping my friend Oliver with a project he's working on."

"Oh, that scrawny freshman?" she asked curiously.

"Yes," I said in surprise. "You've met him?"

"Yeah." She nodded. "Jeremiah's had him over a few times." She shrugged. "I thought it was an odd friendship, but now I understand."

"Why's that?" I teased her. "Is it because he's my friend? Two odd ducks?"

"You're not odd." She smiled and touched my shoulder. "And neither is Oliver. I was going to say I understand why

Jeremiah has a new brilliant friend, because you're brilliant as well."

"I'm not brilliant." My face reddened.

"Yes, you are." She bit her lower lip and looked down. "That's why I like you so much."

"You like me?" I said in surprise, my heart racing and explosions going off in my head.

"Yes." She nodded, shyly.

"But what about Jeremiah?"

She shrugged in response, and I saw a pink hue in her cheeks. I was about to ask her if she wanted to go on a date with me when Jeremiah approached us.

"How are my best girl and my best friend?" Jeremiah grinned as he offered us two champagne glasses.

"Good." I nodded and took the glass from him, frustrated that he'd interrupted before I'd had the chance to ask Angelina exactly what she'd meant.

"Not drinking?" Jeremiah frowned at Angelina as she turned down the drink and gave him her cheek as he leaned down to kiss her.

"Not tonight." She shook her head slightly and gave me a look.

"So, nice party," I said to Jeremiah. "Not afraid your neighbors will complain?"

"Nope." He laughed. "My godfather owns the building, and my uncle is best friends with the police chief. I think we'll be okay."

"It must be nice to have friends in high places," I said to him, and he laughed.

"You should know, right?" He winked and then looked at Angelina. "You okay, babe? You look a bit pale."

"I'm fine." She nodded. "Just tired."

"Oh, that's not good. I have coke, if you want some. Give you the pep you need."

"No, no, that's fine." She shook her head quickly. "I'll be fine."

"Jeremiah." A sharp voice squealed. "Jeremiah." The voice grew louder, and I saw Macy Vanderbilt headed toward us. Macy was a prissy blue blood who could trace her ancestry back to the *Mayflower*, and she very much wanted to be with Jeremiah.

"Yes, Macy?" He turned to her with a small smile. Macy was an ice-cold princess, but she was also gorgeous with her long blond hair and clear blue eyes.

"Why is Joanie Rosenberg here?" She turned her nose up at Angelina and me as she talked to Jeremiah. "How can you have the cafeteria girl at your party?"

"Everyone is welcome at my parties, Macy," Jeremiah said with a tight smile. That wasn't the only place everyone was welcome in Jeremiah's life. Macy and Joanie were both welcome in his bed as well. He'd been sleeping with them for the last six months, and I had no idea how he was stringing them both along. I also had no idea if Angelina knew he was cheating on her, and as much as I wanted to let it slip, that would be a fatal blow to our friendship. I still felt bound by a certain honor and respect for Jeremiah, even if I didn't agree with his actions—and even if I wanted Angelina for myself. As much as I wanted Angelina, Jeremiah was still my friend. Sure, he was a spoiled, superior brat, but deep down he was a good guy. He'd been there for me in ways that I could never thank him for. And I appreciated that he treated me like an equal— unlike Larry, who only seemed to tolerate me for Jeremiah's benefit. We were an odd group of friends, and I often wondered what would happen when we graduated.

"Well, I don't think she should be here." Macy made a face. "She's not our kind of people."

"Who is your kind of people?" I asked her curiously, knowing she didn't particularly care for me either. Macy didn't deign to answer me. Instead, she just looked both Angelina and me up and down distastefully and then turned back to Jeremiah. I didn't care if Macy hated me, and I always spoke up for Joanie. Joanie had had a crush on me before she'd started sleeping with Jeremiah, and I'd always felt guilty for not reciprocating.

"Jeremiah, can we go to your room?" She rubbed his back. "I need to tell you something in private."

"Oh?" Jeremiah looked at her with a bored expression.

"Yes." She licked her lips slowly, and I watched as she slipped a finger into her mouth. "I need to tell you something very badly."

"Well, okay then." Jeremiah grinned as he realized that what Macy had to tell him had less to do with talking and more to do with sucking, a fact that was unmistakable to all three of us standing there. "I'll see you guys in a bit," Jeremiah said with a quick smile, and he and Macy walked away. I looked over at Angelina to see if she was upset, but she just gave me a sweet smile and laughed. I raised an eyebrow at her, and she whispered in my ear.

"I'm not a dumbo, Nicholas. Maybe I have my own reasons for dating Jeremiah."

"Oh?" I looked at her with a frown. Was she just interested in his money?

"Maybe it was the only way I could get to hang out with you." She winked, and my heart stopped beating. Was she kidding? "Want to get out of here?" she asked softly, and I nodded, not quite believing my good luck. Was Angelina Walker really interested in me? We headed toward the front door of the apartment, and I saw Oliver standing there looking at us with a frown as we were about to leave.

"Where are you two going?" he questioned us in an aggressive tone. Oliver looked stiff and out of place at the party, and a part of me wondered what else I could do to help him assimilate a bit better to college life. When I first met him, I'd assumed that he was a younger version of me and that once he made friends he'd lose his awkwardness, but that never happened. Instead, he seemed to be odder than ever. And he seemed to have become closer to Jeremiah than he was to me.

"We're skipping out." I smiled at him. "Want to come?"

"What do you mean? This is Jeremiah's party." He looked angry. "You can't leave. Not until the party ends."

"We're bored," Angelina said, and flipped her hair. "Why don't you come with us? We can go to Harvard Square."

"You shouldn't be going anywhere with Nick," Oliver said accusingly. "You're Jeremiah's girlfriend."

"Not anymore." She laughed.

"Since when?" He blinked rapidly.

"Since now." She put her arm through mine and kissed me on the cheek.

"Nick?" Oliver's eyes widened.

"Yes?" I couldn't stop myself from beaming.

"Jeremiah's your friend."

"And he's in the bedroom with Macy," I snapped, annoyed that Oliver was trying to make me feel bad. "Look, we're leaving. Are you coming or not?"

"No." He looked disappointed. "I'm not leaving Jeremiah Bradley's big party, and you shouldn't be either." I felt sad as I listened to him talking. He said Jeremiah's name in such a reverential way that it broke my heart. Maybe I would have been better off leaving Oliver in the lab by himself that day. He seemed to idolize Jeremiah in a way that wasn't healthy.

"Well, have fun, Oliver," Angelina said sweetly. "Let's go, Nicholas."

"Bye, Oliver," I said, and followed Angelina out of the party. As soon as the door closed behind us, we ran down the hallway and scrambled down the stairs. Bursting onto the pavement in front of Jeremiah's apartment, we giggled as we stared at each other. We stood there for a few moments, just taking each other in. Angelina's face was bright and cheery, her sparkling hazel eyes glowing green as the streetlights lit the side of her face. Her lips were pink and luscious, and her long brown hair shone like spun silk. She had such a look of happiness on her face that I couldn't help grinning back at her.

"I'm so glad Jeremiah had this party," she said finally.

"Why's that?" I asked softly.

"Because I got to leave with you."

"Are you sure you want to do this?" I asked, and took her hand. "Jeremiah might be mad."

"I'm sure. What about you?"

"I'm positive," I said steadily, and grinned.

"So you do like me?" She cocked her head as she stared at me. "I wasn't sure."

"Oh, I more than like you. I love you," I said, and then I groaned. I wasn't sure why I'd told her I loved her. It was uncool, and I was scared that she'd think I was a psychopath.

"You love me?" She raised an eyebrow at me and then giggled.

"You think I'm a loser now, don't you?"

"No," she said shyly, and stepped toward me. "I think you're sweet."

"Really?" I asked doubtfully.

"Really." She kissed me lightly on the lips. "You're sweet. And I kinda think I might love you as well."

"But you don't even know me." I frowned.

"I know you as well as you know me," she said lightly, and I touched the side of her face.

"He's going to be pissed, you know." I sighed as I gazed at her. I knew Jeremiah didn't love Angelina, but he saw her as a conquest, and he wouldn't be happy to lose her.

"He'll be fine." She laughed. "What's the worst he can do?"

"True, he can move on to other girls." I nodded, but there was a fear in my stomach that wouldn't go away. What would Jeremiah try to do? For some reason, I had a feeling that it wouldn't be as simple as we hoped. I could only hope that he would move on with his life and just forget that Angelina was the one that got away.

four

Bianca London
Present Day

"Let's go somewhere." Steve stepped back after replacing his flask in his pocket.

"Go?" I asked him. Was he out of his mind? Did he think I was going anywhere with him? "With you?"

"Yeah." He nodded, unblinking. "I had a thought." He looked over at Rosie. "Maybe now is the time?"

"I think so." Rosie nodded, her eyes narrowed.

"The time for what?" My voice rose. What were they going to do to me? Where did they want me to go? "I thought you said you only wanted to make sure I saw the tape. Why do I have to go anywhere with you?"

"Bianca, there's someone we want you to meet." Rosie pursed her lips. "You need to come with us."

"No one the two of you know is someone I want to meet," I said scathingly, though I was starting to panic. What were they planning? I tried to imagine what Jakob would advise in this situation. He'd tell me to stay calm, take a deep breath. He'd tell me not to let them see my fear. I felt my heartbeat slowing as I pictured his face and imagined him speaking to me reassuringly.

"Can't you ever just listen?" Rosie looked annoyed, and then her voice softened as she looked at me. "Please, Bianca."

"Please? You think that means anything to me?" I looked at her haughtily, my eyes expressing my complete and utter disdain for her. "We were best friends, Rosie. I don't know how you, in good conscience, can even look me in the eyes right now, you Judas."

"*I'm* the Judas?" She leaned her head back and laughed. The sound was hollow and bitter, and it terrified me.

"That is the applicable name for traitors these days." I nodded, and I could see that Steve was uncomfortable with our conversation. "We've been friends for years, Rosie. How could you do this to me?"

"Oh, stop being a frightened little rabbit, Bianca. It's not becoming." Rosie turned away from me, but I could see that her face was reddening. I was getting to her in some way.

"Has my friendship always meant nothing to you?" I asked softly, and thought back to our days in college. Had it all been a lie? I thought about the first day we'd met. I'd been lugging two bags of laundry across campus so that I could go to a Laundromat. I hadn't thought the washers and dryers located in the dorm room were doing a good enough job.

Rosie had appeared out of nowhere to help me, as one of my bags had exploded and clothes had gone everywhere.

"It's a good thing I was here to help you," she'd said with a confident smile as she'd helped gather my clothes into a big black plastic bag she'd been carrying. To this day, I'm still not sure what she was doing with that plastic bag.

"Yes, thank you," I'd said gratefully as we'd scooped my clothes up.

"Imagine if a guy had seen you with all these Mickey Mouse granny panties?" She'd giggled as she held a pair up. "You'd never find a boyfriend," she'd continued, and my face had burned with shame. I think she'd noticed that I was upset because she'd touched my shoulder lightly. "Not that it matters. You're so pretty that most guys won't even care." And of course that had made me forget her bitchy comment. That had been par for the course during our whole friendship, if I was honest. She'd diss me, or say something hurtful, but then she'd be such a good friend that I'd forgive her for the quips. Now that I was thinking back on it, it hadn't been the best friendship. There had been so many signs that Rosie didn't actually like me very much. I couldn't believe that I'd been so blind.

"Bianca." Steve stood in front of me. His manic eyes looked worried. "We need to leave now." I stared back at him, my heart pounding, and then I looked at Rosie, her face impassive as she stood there. And then my phone rang—I was never more thankful for a ringing phone. Never in my life. I glanced at the screen and saw Jakob's name flashing on it. The room went quiet as we all stared at my ringing phone.

"We need to leave. Now," Rosie said as soon as my phone stopped ringing. "Grab her, Steve. We need to get out of here."

"Steve, don't." I shook my head at him. What were they planning on doing to me? Then my phone started ringing again, and Jakob's name flashed on the screen again, and I grinned inwardly. *Thank you, Jakob.* "Jakob keeps calling. He's not going to stop. And if I don't answer the phone soon, he's going to be worried," I said as I glanced down at my ringing phone again. "He'll be suspicious if I don't pick up soon and even more so if I don't go home." I watched as Steve and Rosie looked at each other searchingly. They didn't know what to do. They knew that if I left with them, Jakob would be hot on their trail. "I should answer," I said and brought the phone up to my face.

"Don't." Rosie turned to me with a grimace. "Just be quiet while we think, Bianca."

"Excuse me?" I stared at Rosie. "Who do you think—"

"Bianca." Rosie sighed in exasperation. "Please." Her eyes widened in frustration, and my heart sank slightly as we just stared at each other. A wave of sadness passed over me as I gazed at her familiar blond hair and pretty, yet hard, face.

"What should we do?" Steve looked at Rosie, and I could see that she was thinking deeply. I studied them casually. How long had Rosie been working with Steve? Did David know? My head started pounding as I thought about all the double-crossing that was going on. Was anyone trustworthy? I knew that of everyone I knew, my college friend Blake was someone

I could absolutely trust to help me and Jakob. He had already proven himself to be a true friend when he'd researched the Bradley family for me. He had no agenda in this whole situation. If only I'd told Blake where I was going, maybe he could have helped me. Maybe I could have brought him with me? Why had I hurried over here by myself? I was so annoyed at the amateur mistakes I was making, like some dumb chick in a horror movie. Had I learned nothing from my slasher-movie-marathon weekend? A twinge of guilt ran through me as I thought about Jakob. I should have told him as well. He'd think I'd come because I lost faith in him again. He'd think we were back at square one, but we weren't. Not really. I'd just acted without thinking. Now I wished I'd told both of them. There was no way Steve and Rosie could have overpowered all three of us. The phone stopped ringing and then immediately started again, and I held it up for them to see.

"It's Jakob again," I said softly. "He's going to come looking for me if I don't answer. He's going to come looking for me, and if he doesn't find me, you two are going to be the prime suspects. What do you think he's going to do when he finds out that you've taken me?" My heart warmed as I spoke, for I was sure the words were true. I knew that Jakob was desperately worried and I'd never been more grateful for his overprotective ways as I was when that phone kept on ringing.

"Don't be such a stupid bitch, Bianca." Rosie's voice cracked. "I have tried to keep this in all these years, but you are the most ungrateful, most idiotic little . . ." Her voice rose, and she stepped toward me with her eyes spewing hate and her hands in the air. "I'm not going to hit you," she spat out as I cringed. "You're pathetic, aren't you? He bloody kidnapped you, but he's the one you trust?"

"What are you talking about?"

"Jakob kidnapped you. You *knew* he kidnapped you, yet when you came back, you trusted him more than you trusted me. And I was your best friend."

"I didn't trust him more than I trusted you," I said, but I knew that was a lie. At the end of the day, I had never let Rosie in. I'd never let her know my plans to infiltrate Bradley Inc., I'd never really told her about my investigations. I'd never let her in too deeply, and when I'd come back, I still hadn't told her everything. I bit down on my lower lip as I realized that some instinctive, subconscious part of me had been wary of telling her too much. Had I known that she was bad without every really acknowledging it?

"You're like your mother," she said, her blue eyes cold. "So nicey-nicey, but inside you're a fake."

"My mother?"

"Yes, your mother. My mom told me all about her. The games she used to play. She used to pretend she was the perfect little angel. Angelic Angelina that all the men wanted." Rosie scoffed. "If it wasn't for her . . ." Her voice trailed off, and she looked at Steve. Steve was also frowning, and he looked at me.

"If it wasn't for your mother, none of us would be here," Rosie concluded.

"What are you talking about?" I shouted. "You didn't even know my mom. My mom was a good person."

"Your mom was a gold-digging whore," Rosie said with such venom that I knew that she had a real hatred for me and my family.

"My mom was not a whore!" I said, my voice cracking. "Maybe she made a mistake by sleeping with Jeremiah, but she wasn't a whore."

"She was Jeremiah's girlfriend," Steve said. "She was with him before she started dating your dad."

"What?" My jaw dropped.

"It was because of your mom that Jeremiah did what he did." Steve clenched his fists. "If your mom hadn't left Jeremiah for Nick, then he never would have set everything up. My father wouldn't have ended up being the casualty in the middle."

"Bianca, your dad made both my father and Steve's collateral damage," Rosie said. "He ruined lives, and now, in effect, so have you."

"So now you want to ruin mine?" I said softly. "I'm not my mother. What have I done to you?"

"We don't want to ruin your life, Bianca." Steve shook his head. "We want to help you. We want to help you get revenge on the men that ruined all of our lives."

"The men?" My head was pounding and I just wanted to tell them to stop for a few minutes. I needed to think about what they were saying.

"Jakob and David Bradley," Rosie said, and looked at me. "We want to bring them down."

"David as well?" My eyes narrowed as I stared at Rosie. "You love David."

"I do?" She shook her head and looked at me sympathetically. "You think I could love a man that tries to sleep with every two-bit whore he meets?" She looked me up and down. "You think I could love a man that tried to sleep with you?"

"But . . ." My voice trailed off. So Rosie didn't love David. Did that mean she was playing him as well? I stared at her beautiful face and marveled at what a good actress she was. She could have made it big in Hollywood. I was pretty certain she had fooled both me and David.

"Bianca, it will all be explained if you come with us," Steve said. "Someone's after you. Someone we want you to see before he sees you."

"Who?" I asked in confusion. Who was it that they wanted me to see so badly?

"We can't tell you." Rosie walked away and muttered something under her breath that I couldn't hear.

"Jakob is going to wonder where I am if I don't call him or go back home." I said his name again, wanting them to remember that it wasn't just me.

"Do you really trust him, Bianca? None of the Bradleys are to be trusted," Rosie said. "Don't you understand that? Yes, he's handsome and charming, but what does that really mean? Nothing, Bianca. It means nothing. You need to stick with the people who have been trying to help you. Listen to Steve and me."

"Okay," I said, and nodded slowly. She didn't know it, but her words confirmed to me that I could trust Jakob. If he had anything to do with this, she wouldn't be advocating so hard for me not to trust him. I knew without a doubt that when it came to trusting Steve and Rosie or to trusting Jakob, that Jakob had my trust every single time. Even though I still didn't know what I'd seen in the video or what was going on or what David had been talking about. Why had Jakob tied David up? Why had David said that once I found out the truth I would leave Jakob? What truth was I supposed to find out? And why had they been discussing my father's death?

I just didn't understand what I'd seen in the video at all. The only thing I knew for certain was that Jakob and David were not working together. There had been way too much hostility between them for that to be the case—the video practically crackled with intensity. And even though I didn't always understand Jakob's motivations, when it came down to it, he'd always protected me. He wasn't going to hurt me. And in that moment, I knew that I couldn't let them know that. "So what do you want me to do?"

Rosie nodded and smiled as she gazed at me. "I knew you'd come to your senses."

"Yes, you know me, Rosie. A little ditzy." I stood there with a small smile, but I could tell she was still a little suspicious. "I always have bad luck choosing men. You know that." I made a face and stepped toward her. "But I do remember how you've always been there for me, taking me for drinks and tacos." I rubbed her shoulder. "You were a good friend to me, Rosie. I won't forget that. You're right, you're the one I should have been trusting this whole time. I don't know why I was so dumb as to have not told you everything from the beginning." I almost choked on the lies.

"Go and see Jakob so you can reassure him you're okay," Rosie said with a flip of her blond hair. Steve looked angry at her decision, and she continued. "This is for the best. This way Jakob will think she still trusts him. This way we can get him where we want him."

"So what do I do?"

"The Masquerade Ball is on Saturday," Rosie said, and looked at me with a small smile. "You both need to come."

"The Bradley Ball?" I frowned. I'd been there once before, and I didn't know that I really wanted to go back again.

"Yes." She nodded. "It's the perfect place for us to have some anonymity while still in a public place."

"And I'll meet whoever it is you want us to meet."

"Yes." She nodded with a small smile. "You'll meet whoever it is we want you to meet."

"You're not going to tell me?"

"Don't you like surprises?"

"Will I be surprised?"

"Well, I'm sure Jakob will be surprised, even if you're not."

"Why?"

"Because in life there is death and in death there is life," Rosie said, and turned to Steve. "Let's go."

"Go?" It was Steve's turn to look surprised. "I thought we were going to take Bianca with us."

"Now isn't a good time." Rosie shook her head. "This is better for *us*."

"But he said to bring her to him." Steve looked worried.

"This is better for *us*, Steve." She reached over and touched his arm. "We'll all get our revenge on the Bradleys." She looked at me. "We'll avenge all the wrongs that have been done to all of us. He's not going to dictate what we do, Steve. He couldn't have done any of this without you. He needs you. And when it's time, we'll bring him down as well."

"But . . ." Steve's eyes were wide, and he looked at me.

"What does it matter if she knows?" Rosie shrugged. "She'll know soon enough. She's a part of it as well. She can help avenge her mother. It will be poetic justice. All of the Bradleys destroyed." She laughed and threw her head back. "And then we can claim what is ours. You can claim what is yours. You can finally have everything your father worked so hard for. You should have been running that company. You were Jeremiah's bitch boy. His slave. Now it's your turn, Steve. It's your turn to make him your bitch."

My heart thudded as they stared at each other. They had an odd connection. Rosie seemed to be able to reach a part of Steve that I certainly hadn't while on the island. Even though they were letting me go, I felt uneasy. Really uneasy. I didn't know what they were talking about. Who was the big "he" that they were referring to? Who did they want me to meet? Who else was a part of this?

"Be at the ball on Saturday." Rosie turned to me. "You and Jakob."

"I'll be there." I nodded, and as surreptitiously as they had entered, they left. I stood there feeling faint and clutched my phone to me for a few seconds before it began ringing again. I was about to answer and tell Jakob what had just happened, but it was Blake calling me. "Hello?" I said, my voice weak.

"Bianca," he said hurriedly. "We need to talk."

"Okay," I said, and swallowed hard. My legs were trembling, and my whole body was shaking in some sort of post-traumatic shock. "What's going on?"

"I found some new files. It's funny what databases you can link to at the library." He sounded excited. "The world is literally at your fingertips. So much access to so many different things—"

"Blake."

"Sorry, you know how excited I get," he said, and his voice dropped. "Can you meet me at a café in five minutes? I don't want to tell you anything over the phone."

"Um, depends. What café?" I said, wondering what had him so excited. "What's going on, Blake? You're freaking me out."

"Did you know that there is no death certificate for Jeremiah Bradley?" His voice was a whisper, which almost made me laugh because if our phones were being tapped, his dropping his voice wasn't going to make it so they couldn't hear. I was pretty sure that if I could understand what he was saying, anyone tapping our phones could also understand.

"Okay?" I said, wondering what the big deal was. And then my head started thudding as I thought back to what Steve and Rosie had just been saying. It wasn't possible, was it? "Where do you want to meet?"

"Text me when you get to a coffee shop," he said. "I'll meet you wherever you go."

"Okay." My voice dropped now, and I whispered, "You're not saying what I think you're saying, are you?"

"I don't know what you think I'm saying, but if you're also thinking that there's a new Maestro Geppetto in town, then yes." He cleared his throat. "Well, not new. I think this puppeteer has been here all along."

five

Nicholas London
Decades Ago

"I'm worried about Oliver, Nick." Angelina's brow furrowed as I walked toward her in the small kitchen. I stared at the concern on her face, and my stomach twisted. "I think you need to reach out to him. I don't think his friendship with Jeremiah is good for him."

"Why?" I tried not to express my annoyance. I didn't want to talk about Oliver or any of my friends, least of all Jeremiah.

"I just don't think Jeremiah is a great friend to him." She picked up a loaf of French bread and offered it to me. "Do you want some bread and butter?"

"I wouldn't say no." I smiled. "Do you have any cheese as well?"

"I have some Brie." She nodded and smiled. "Sit and I'll cut it."

"You spoil me." I sat down willingly and waited for my

pre-dinner snack. Angelina and I had been dating for just over six months now, and we'd already gotten into a comfortable routine. She took care of me well.

"I do, but you spoil me too." She started humming. "I can't believe we're going to go see a show in New York City."

"I can't believe you've never seen a show in the city before. We're not that far away."

"But I moved here from Florida." She laughed. "I haven't had an opportunity to go to the city before. I was going to go see *Les Miz* with my roommates, but then Jeremiah wanted to take me. . . ." Her voice trailed off. "Sorry."

"There's no need to be sorry." I shrugged, but a pang of guilt hit me. My friendship with Jeremiah was definitely different now. The whole dynamic in our group had completely changed. Jeremiah and Larry were always together and did things without inviting me. Which wasn't altogether irregular, as they had known each other for a long time. However, they were also including Oliver, which was weird. It was obviously an unsubtle hint that I was no longer in the inner circle, and while that hurt, I didn't know what to do. I had broken the brotherly code. I had taken Jeremiah's girl. Though we both knew that she wasn't really his girl.

"I know, but I still feel bad." Angelina sighed. "I don't trust Jeremiah. I still suspect he has some sort of ulterior motive. He's not really a good guy. He just plays his role really well."

"I think he's fine," I said, not really sure if I meant my words. Jeremiah hadn't made me an outcast exactly, but he

had made comments, almost threats, that had me wondering
what he was really thinking. I hadn't told Angelina about any
of that, of course. I hadn't wanted to upset her. And I didn't
want her to start feeling guilty and leave me. All I cared about
besides my schoolwork was being with her. She was my life. I
couldn't imagine losing her. I knew I was being dramatic, far
more dramatic than I'd ever thought I could be, but I suppose love and relationships can twist anyone's mind. We're all
capable of losing it over someone we love.

"His parents are powerful." She bit her lower lip. "And
Larry . . ." She made a face. Angelina couldn't stand Larry. "I
trust him even less than I trust Jeremiah. He just seems like
an opportunist, and I think he might even be a psychopath."

"Psychopath?"

"Or sociopath?" She shrugged her shoulders. "What's the
name for people that can harm others and feel nothing bad
about it?"

"Yes, that's a sociopath. They don't feel any remorse after
their actions."

"I wish that Brigitta would stop seeing Larry." Angelina
made a sad face. "We barely talk anymore."

"I know, and I'm sorry." I stood up and held her to me.
"I guess I didn't think about the repercussions of us dating."

"I don't think either of us did." Angelina rubbed my
head. "I feel like I'm in some sort of Russian novel."

"You're not in a novel." I laughed. "We're just in college. There are no spies and no hidden agendas." I kissed
her gently on the lips. "When we graduate, none of us will

remember any of this." I kissed her again for emphasis and pulled away as I heard the doorbell ringing. "Who's that?" I asked, confused. It was late, and Angelina hadn't told me of any study plans.

"I invited everyone over for dinner." She smiled guiltily at me.

"You what?" I stepped back and frowned. "Why would you do that?"

"I want to clear the air. I want us all to go back to how we were before it all got awkward."

"Who did you invite?" My stomach churned as I thought about how the night was going to make things even more tense.

"Jeremiah, of course. Larry." She made a face. "Brigitta, Macy, and Oliver."

"Oh." I closed my eyes for a few seconds as the doorbell rang again. "You know this is going to be incredibly awkward, right?"

"I know." She grabbed my hands. "Sorry." She sighed. "I just want you to have your friends back."

"You didn't invite Joanie?"

"No." She looked away from me, and I could see her face flushing. "I didn't."

"Okay." I didn't say anything else, though I was upset. I liked Joanie. I considered her a friend. She was like me, in a way. Her parents were poor, yet she didn't let that stop her from doing what she wanted to do. I knew that Angelina was jealous of my friendship with Joanie and didn't understand that I just felt her to be a kindred spirit. I didn't think about her romantically. I didn't want her in my bed, but I knew that Angelina didn't understand. Jealousy was such a base emotion. It was hard to control, even when rationally you knew there was nothing to be worried about.

"I can call her now if you want," she said softly, her hazel eyes looking into mine with an expression of love and worry. My heart melted as I gazed into her beautiful face. I didn't understand how she could think, for even one minute, that my heart could ever belong to another.

"No." I shook my head. "Tonight will be crazy enough as it is. Besides, Macy doesn't like Joanie."

"Yeah." Angelina rolled her eyes. "Though I don't know who she is to be so high and mighty. He cheated on me with both of them."

"Yeah, well . . ." My voice trailed off. I didn't want to tell Angelina what a bad idea I thought this was. I didn't want to upset her, as I knew she was only trying. But now that Jeremiah was dating Macy, she had gotten even snobbier, and I knew that she, like Larry, didn't understand why Jeremiah still kept me around. And I wasn't sure what was going on with Oliver. He barely spoke to me anymore. "I'll get the door." I made a face. "I guess I know why you got the Brie now."

"Am I that transparent?" She giggled. "We can't eat it all though. I promised my roommate that I'd save her some. It was the only way I could convince her to leave the apartment for the entire evening."

"Well, aren't we lucky that Sue is easily bribed with food.

Just imagine how much more colorful tonight could have been." I laughed. "Especially if Sue tried to do a séance."

"She only does that with people she's met at least twice." Angelina giggled, and we both sighed as the doorbell rang again.

"Here goes," I said as I walked to the door with a heavy heart. I really, really didn't want to deal with the drama that I knew was going to ensue this evening, but I'd do it for Angelina. I'd do absolutely anything for Angelina; such was my love for her.

~

"Very good meal. Thank you, Angelina." Jeremiah sat back at the table and rubbed his stomach. "Your cooking reminds me of my aunty Mabel's cooking. Reminiscent of the food I used to get in the South."

"Aunty Mabel?" Macy looked confused. "Who is she? What side of the family?" She interrogated Jeremiah. "I don't remember seeing her in your family tree."

"Aunty Mabel was his nanny," Larry answered for Jeremiah. "She was also his father's nanny, so he called her Aunty. I know this because I asked him why he was calling her Aunty when I came to stay with his family in the summers."

"Larry was wondering why I had an older black lady for an aunt." Jeremiah burst out laughing. "I told him that we were related by blood as well, but he never believed me."

"I thought you were joking. . . ." Larry looked at Jeremiah in confusion.

"No." Jeremiah shook his head. "Not really. Mabel's mother and my grandfather used to knock boots, so to speak."

"What?" Larry leaned forward. "So you have—"

"Guess the apple doesn't fall far from the tree," Angelina cut Larry off, and gave Jeremiah a pertinent look. "Weren't your grandparents married for sixty years?"

"Yes, so?" Jeremiah looked cool as a cucumber as he raised one eyebrow and looked at her with a small smile.

"So he was cheating on his wife."

"*Cheating* is such a crass term." Jeremiah shrugged. "Women should know their place."

"Like Joanie Rosenberg?" Angelina said, and I could see that she was getting angry.

"Angelina," Brigitta spoke up, and I looked at her in surprise. She'd been silent most of the evening, and she and Larry weren't in each other's laps as they usually were.

"What? I'm just asking a question."

"We're not dating anymore, Angelina," Jeremiah said softly. "I don't have to answer all of your questions. You left me for my best friend, remember?"

"Jeremiah," I said, and stared at him. "If you want to talk to me, we can, but don't make out like this is Angelina's fault."

"I don't think it's Angelina's fault." He shook his head, and his eyes narrowed as he looked at me. "I think that life sorts things out as they are supposed to be."

"What does that mean?" I frowned. I hated it when

Jeremiah spoke theoretically and philosophically. I was a science guy. I wanted to deal with tangible facts.

"Just that everything works out how it is supposed to." Jeremiah smiled. "We are all expendable, and that is life."

"What they did was wrong," Oliver said. Jeremiah shook his head and turned away from him. "I would never do that to you. I would never—"

"Go and get me another beer, Oliver." Jeremiah finally spoke as he dismissed the thin young boy.

"Okay." Oliver stood up, his face sullen as he glared at me.

"I'll come with you." Angelina stood up, and I watched as Brigitta jumped up as well and they all walked into the kitchen.

"Are you really going to keep being a dick, Jeremiah?" I said finally, and I heard Larry gasp.

"Me, a dick?" He laughed. "Do you think I really care that you're dating Angelina? She's a frigid bitch. Good luck with that."

"I'm not going to hit you, because you deserve to get one dig in," I said in a low voice. "But if you ever say anything like that again, I will smack all the teeth out of your mouth. I might be just a nerdy scientist, but I've got a mean right hook."

"Wow." Jeremiah surprised me by grinning, his eyes lighting up in respect. "Where has this Nicholas London been all my life?"

"What do you mean?" Larry said, annoyed. "Aren't you going to punch him?"

"No." Jeremiah laughed. "Only commoners resort to laying hands on each other."

"I'm a commoner." I nodded and glared at them both.

"We know," Larry said, and Jeremiah touched him on the shoulder.

"Calm down, Larry. It's fine." Jeremiah looked at me and reached his hand out. "Truce?"

"I never had any problems with you."

"Good." Jeremiah nodded. "Plus the two of you make a great couple. Beauty and charm."

"Beauty and charm?" I asked with a confused expression.

"She's beautiful and you're charming. It's a perfect combination," Jeremiah said with a straight face. "You both deserve each other."

"Okay, well I'm glad to hear that you don't hate me." I nodded slowly, not really sure if he'd been complimenting or dissing me.

"That wouldn't be good if three business partners started off hating each other."

"Business partners?" Larry and I frowned. "What are you talking about?"

"We're graduating soon." Jeremiah smiled. "And I've got a trust fund that needs to be spent. I want us to start a company together. Nick's got the engineering skills; Larry, you can become our attorney once you finish with law school; and I'll be the CEO and in charge of the money."

"I don't know." I shook my head, my brain reeling with this offer. "What would we do?"

"We'd create new products." Jeremiah nodded. "That's what you and Oliver like doing, right, Nick?"

"Well, we like experimenting," I agreed. "But I've not really created anything yet."

"What about the self-painter that Oliver's working on?" Jeremiah said casually.

"Oliver's going to be a partner too?" Larry looked annoyed.

"Of course not." Jeremiah shook his head. "We'll be Bradley, London, and Maxwell. Oliver can work for us."

"I don't know," I said, not really sure what to think of his idea. "Is everything forgiven?"

"There's nothing to forgive," Jeremiah said with a magnanimous smile. "We're brothers. Brothers are always there for each other."

"I guess so," I said doubtfully. I wasn't sure what Angelina was going to make of this new development, but maybe she'd be happy. She was the one that had arranged this whole dinner.

"Just promise me one thing." Jeremiah leaned forward, his eyes sparkling like blue sapphires.

"What's that?"

"If you ever come up with a way to live forever, let me be the first one you tell." Jeremiah grinned.

"You want to live forever?"

"Doesn't everyone?" He rubbed his hands together. "I never want to die. I want to rule the world. I want to be a king. A champion. I want to be everlasting."

"Your legacy could be everlasting," I said. "I'm not sure that I can promise you a way to live forever."

"Don't worry about it." He grinned. "I'll think of a way."

"If anyone can do it, you can," Larry said loyally.

"That is true." Jeremiah sat back and grinned to himself. I stared at him in silence and wondered what was going through his brain. Many times I'd stared at Jeremiah and wondered exactly who he was. I didn't think even Larry knew the real Jeremiah. Jeremiah Bradley was an enigma. But if there was anyone that could find a way to live forever, it would be him.

six

Bianca London
Present Day

There's a French movie called *Jules et Jim*. It was a hard movie for me to follow when I first watched it, but the story was so delicately complex that I watched it a second time. And I realized for all its simplicity, it was a touching and crazy roller-coaster ride. The story is an emotional tale of love, lust, friendship, betrayal, and hurt, and ultimately when it ends, it leaves you wondering what just happened. On a very base level, it's a movie about two best friends who fall in love with the same girl. On a much deeper level, it's about the things we do to keep the ones we love.

The first time I watched the movie, I was annoyed, because to me everything in life is black-and-white. You either love someone or you don't. And if you love someone, that's it. That was your one true love, that was your soul mate. There were no shades of gray, no in-between.

No "he might be the one or he might not be." And certainly there was no loving two men at the same time. It just wasn't possible. But now—now I know that everything in life isn't black-and-white. Falling in love and loving someone aren't the be-all and end-all of life either. The idea of having one true love is something we tell ourselves to make our lives easier. Soul mates and destinies are the things of fairy tales. Unfortunately, I'm not a kid anymore. I don't believe in Prince Charming and riding off into the sunset. I'm a much more practical girl. Being in love with someone doesn't always mean letting down your guard 100 percent.

"Where were you?" Jakob's voice was accusing as I let myself into his apartment. His eyes looked worried, and my heart stilled for a few seconds as I took in his appearance. He rushed over to me, his eyes searching mine. His hair was messy, and his hands were clenched as I looked up at him with a weak smile. His eyes narrowed as he surveyed my face and he pulled me into his arms and kissed the top of my forehead tenderly. "I was worried about you, Bianca. I thought someone had come and taken you."

"I was out," I said lightly, not wanting to get into a long, drawn-out conversation. And not wanting to give him a reason to tell me I was stupid to have gone out by myself without telling him. I knew I was lucky that Steve and Rosie had let me go, but I was too tired and confused to talk about it right now. I just needed time to think and sort things out in my mind before talking more to Jakob. My meeting with

Blake hadn't happened. I'd waited at the coffee shop for about thirty minutes before he'd called me and told me he couldn't come. I'd asked him what it was he'd wanted to tell me, but he'd said he couldn't tell me over the phone. I was worried that someone had gotten to him, but hadn't known what else to do. He'd said to keep my phone close to me and he'd call me again later.

"Out where?" He walked toward me and grabbed my hands. "I've been worried out of my mind. You didn't answer my calls."

"Sorry, I was otherwise engaged." I sighed, sat down on his couch, and leaned back and rubbed my forehead to try to get rid of the dull headache that had taken over my head.

"Doing what?" He sat down next to me, and I looked up into his eyes. He looked stressed out, and I realized how selfish I had been by not calling him back when I'd gone to meet Blake.

"I was watching a video of you, actually," I said softly, and grimaced slightly as I recalled the video of Jakob and his brother. I'd almost forgotten about that, what with Steve and Rosie showing up.

"A video of me?" His dark blue eyes narrowed, and something flashed across his face as he gazed at me. "What was I doing in the video?"

"What do you think you were doing?" I pursed my lips and sighed as I gazed up at him. "What's going on, Jakob? What was David talking about when you had him ti—" I said, and he cut me off before I could finish talking.

"So I've been condemned before trial?" His voice was rough as he looked at me sadly. "Are you playing judge, jury, and executioner?"

"Jakob, you're misunderstanding me. You don't even know what I saw." I placed a hand on his shoulder.

"I don't care what you saw." He shrugged my hand off him. "At this point in our relationship, it doesn't matter. At this point in our relationship, there shouldn't be anything I have to worry about or anything you have to worry about. If we see or hear something that looks crazy, we shouldn't automatically judge the other person and think that they are in the wrong." He was getting angrier as he spoke. "There are two feelings you can live your life by, Bianca: love or fear. What's it going to be?" Jakob's tone was intense as he stared at me. "Am I constantly going to have to worry that you're not going to trust me, and you'll question me and judge me based on every little thing you see and hear?"

"I think one should use common sense as well," I said lightly, and stood up. "Sometimes we can go with love, but other times we have to listen to that fear in our brains. That fear is healthy. That fear can prevent us from entering into situations we shouldn't." I placed my hands on his shoulders and looked into his eyes, allowing him to see that I was holding nothing back.

"So which one of those emotions do you feel when you think of me?" he asked me softly and searchingly. I knew that our entire relationship and future, if there was to be a future, depended on my answer now. "And are those feelings now based on a video you saw of me doing heaven knows what?"

"The question should really be which one of those feelings I'm going to go with, as I feel both of them," I said with a small smile, trying to defuse the situation. "Jakob, smile, you're making me feel like Meryl Streep in *Sophie's Choice*." I shook him gently, and he frowned.

"Are you choosing between me and another man?" His eyes darkened. "Is your decision so difficult that you liken it to the Holocaust? Are you so scared and fearful of me? Have I really given you that much reason to distrust me?"

"Of course I don't think this is like the Holocaust." I frowned as I stared at him. His voice was no longer nonchalant, and I could feel my stomach churning in worry. "You have to understand where I'm coming from."

"Bianca, what do you think of me?" His melancholy tone pierced my heart.

"Oh, Jakob." I grabbed his face and pulled it toward me. "Is there any doubt in your mind? I love you and trust you. From the depths of my heart I trust you. Yes, there are times I don't know what's going on or who you are, but ultimately I don't believe that you're going to harm me or trick me."

"Good." He kissed me hard. "You had me worried there."

"When I was saying 'What's going on?' I wasn't talking about with you." I sighed and shook my head. "There's a lot that's happened since I last saw you."

"Same." He squeezed my hand. "I went to see David."

"I figured." I raised an eyebrow at him. "Did you torture him?"

"That was what you saw in the video?" He looked at me carefully and nodded his head. "I should have known."

"Known what?"

"It was a setup." He sighed. "David texted that he needed to see me urgently. When I arrived, he said that Steve had gone rogue and tied him up, but that he'd left his cell phone on the table. When I arrived, he started shouting at me." He shook his head. "And yes, I did get angry with him."

"What did you do?"

"I didn't kill him," Jakob joked, but I wasn't laughing. "Bianca, what are you thinking?"

"Let me explain," I said, sitting next to him on the couch. "I saw Steve and Rosie."

"Together?" Jakob frowned. "Where were you?"

"I went to see David. I thought if I spoke to him by himself, he might tell me something." I held my hand up, as I could see that Jakob was starting to look angry. "I think he has a soft spot for me. I know you don't think so, but he does."

"Are you fucking joking, Bianca?" Jakob exploded, and he looked at me like I was crazy. "Do you really think David cares what happens to you? How could you go and try to speak to him without telling me? What were you thinking?"

"I don't think he's dumb enough to let something slip if it was you and me. However, if it was just me, well, I thought I'd have a chance. I really think I could have gotten more information." I took a deep breath. "I'm tired, Jakob. I'm tired. I'm scared. I don't know what's going to happen from day to day. I just want my life to go back to normal."

"I understand that," he said softly. "But you can't just go off without me."

"You mean like you did to me?" I retorted, and he clenched his fists.

"What did Steve and Rosie want?" He sat down on the couch. "Why were they together, and why were they in David's apartment?"

"I don't know." I pursed my lips. "I don't have many answers, but we're going to get them soon."

"What do you mean?" He grabbed my hands. His fingers ran across my palms and up my wrists. He stroked my skin softly, and I shifted so that I was leaning into him and our thighs were pressed into each other.

"I love you, Jakob. I love you and I trust you." I looked at him and reached up and stroked the side of his face. "I want you to know that. I want you to know that I'm going with love. When it comes to you, I'm going with love."

"Are you sure?" he said, his eyes searching mine. "Is love enough? After everything we've been through? Are you sure that's enough for you?"

"When I was growing up, my dad used to tell me that he loved my mother more than anything. He gave up everything for my mother. He said he never regretted it. He said that he would have done anything for love. He said that he'd have gone to the ends of the earth for one more day with her." My eyes glazed over as I thought about the passion my father's voice always had when he talked about my mom. "He loved her so much. He said that sometimes he couldn't believe how lucky he'd been that she'd chosen him."

"What was her name?"

"Angelina," I said, and then looked at him. "What was your mom's name?"

"Joanie." He said it proudly. "Never Joan. Always Joanie."

"I like Joanie," I said, and then my heart started pounding. "I know this is going to sound crazy, but I feel like I recognize the name Joanie."

"Oh?" He looked at me closely. "What do you recognize about it?"

"I don't know. I don't remember. It just rings a bell." I sighed. "I'm not really sure why."

"Oh, okay." Jakob nodded, but I could see from his face that he was disappointed.

"I'm sorry. I wish we had this all figured out already." I sighed loudly, feeling the annoyance and frustration throughout my body. "I wish I had gotten to meet your mother. To know the person who could raise a son like you and write such beautiful poems." I reached up and stroked the side of his face. "Why don't you read me another one of her poems?"

"I don't want to depress you."

"They don't depress me. They're beautiful. Love is beautiful; heartbreaking at times, yes, but still beautiful."

"How I love you, Bianca. You do know that, right?"

"Yes." I nodded, and my heart filled with joy at the love in his eyes. "I know that."

"So what else happened? How did you get away from that bastard Steve and Rosie?"

"It was thanks to you, actually. When you kept calling me, I could see that they were getting anxious. So I played upon their anxiety. That's when they decided to let me go and let both of us come to the ball."

"Hmm," Jakob said, and I stared at his face. He looked at me, unconvinced, and I sighed.

"What?" I said, and tried to guess what he was thinking.

"Do you think they really let you go just because I was calling?" He shook his head. "Steve is a bloody maniac, and I doubt he's scared of me, and while I don't know Rosie well, she doesn't seem the sort to be scared of a couple of missed calls either."

"So you think they wanted both of us to come?"

"Yes." He nodded. "Though I don't know why they wouldn't have just asked that of us. Why set me up with David, and why ambush you at David's apartment?"

"I don't know." I chewed on my lower lip nervously. "Do you think we should skip the ball?"

"No way," he said instantly. "However, we will ask Blake to come with us."

"With us? Is that a good idea?"

"Not *with us*, with us. I'll get him onto the invite list and he can arrive separately. I have an idea."

"What idea?"

"It'll be easier to explain when Blake is here. Unless you don't want him to be involved anymore?"

"No, he can help us," I said, and made a small face. "Actually, he was meant to meet me today, but he never showed up, so he said he'd call me later."

"You were going to meet up with him?" Jakob sounded jealous, but I could tell he was trying to play it off.

"He's helping *us*, Jakob. He's a good resource. We weren't meeting for a midafternoon hookup." I tried to joke, but he didn't smile.

"Not funny, Bianca." He shook his head. "From here on out, please let me know where you're going and what you're planning. I think it will be safer for both of us to know what the other is up to." He gave me a hard stare. "I can't protect you if I don't know where you are."

"Jakob, I don't need you to protect me." I rolled my eyes at him, but inside I felt a wave of warmth toward him. How could I ever doubt this man? "And if we're going to be straightforward from here on out, tell me your idea." I raised an eyebrow at him and gave him a hard stare back.

"We'll discuss it when Blake calls you. I need to go over some things first. Now, go and have a shower." He winked at me, and my face heated as I glared at him for blowing me off.

"A shower?" I frowned. "We have so much to figure out. I don't want to shower now."

"Bianca, take a shower. Cool down. Calm down. Then we'll talk. Right now you're still reeling from what just happened. I want us both to have fresh minds when we talk."

"Fine." I rolled my eyes and turned away from him. "Bossy boots."

"I can be bossy if you want me to be."

"I don't want you to be," I muttered under my breath.

"Beautiful as a rose, fragile as a butterfly. I watch her in my window with every sunrise."

"Your mom wrote that as well?" I looked at him in surprise.

"No." He smiled as he gazed at me tenderly. "Those words are my own. I guess I inherited my mother's love of poetry now that I have my own muse."

"You love making me blush."

"Not really." He grabbed me around the waist and pulled me into him. "What I love doing," he spoke gently into my ear, "is making you come."

～❂

"Do you trust me?" Jakob walked toward me with a pair of gold handcuffs in his hand and watched me as I dried my hair with one of his plush white towels. There was a sly smile on his face and a question in his eyes.

"Should I trust you?" I raised an eyebrow in a deliberately seductive way, picking up a brush and combing my hair.

"Maybe. Maybe not." He grabbed my right wrist and pulled me toward him. His fingers gripped my skin tightly, and I swallowed hard as I looked into his eyes. They were full of danger and mischief.

"That's not a very good answer," I said softly, and before he knew what was happening, I grabbed the handcuffs from his hand and held them next to my body.

"What are you going to do?" he growled as he let go of my wrist.

"This," I said with a small smile as I grabbed his left wrist and cuffed it.

"Am I under arrest?" he asked with a mischievious smirk on his face.

"Should you be?" I said, not smiling back. I gave him my sternest look, though it took everything in me to not start giggling. How I wanted this man. How I wanted to show him that I just wasn't some submissive little girl he could boss around. I wanted to show him that I could give him as good as he gave.

"Maybe," he said again, and I could see his chest rising quickly. I hid a smile. He was as excited as I was, and maybe even a little intrigued as to what I was going to do next.

"Take off your pants," I commanded him, my eyes dropping to the front of his jeans.

He looked back at me with laughing eyes, and I squeezed the cuff over his wrist. "Now," I said, and stepped back.

"Shouldn't you cuff us together or cuff me to something?" He cocked his head as he stared at me. "Don't you want to make sure that I don't run away and escape?"

"I don't think you're going to run away," I said lightly, and ran my hands down the front of my body and slowly across my breasts. I saw his eyes narrow as he followed the path of my fingers. "Are you?" I said as I pushed my hand up and squeezed my breasts together.

"No," he agreed, his eyes darker now and no longer laughing. I watched as he reached down and unbuckled his jeans and pulled them off with one hand. He stood there in front of me in a pair of white Calvin Klein briefs and a white shirt. It took everything in me not to reach over, unbutton his shirt, and then pull his hardening cock out.

"Take your shirt off now," I said, and this time I hardened my voice. I was playing a role now, and he had to know I meant business. "Hurry!" I snapped as he slowly unbuttoned his shirt. "I don't have all day."

"Neither do I," he said, and I frowned at his tone. Jakob still thought he was calling the shots here. I smiled to myself as I realized how quickly I was going to show him he was wrong.

"Once you've taken your shirt off, go and get me one of the chairs from your dining room." I barely looked at him. Instead I concentrated on brushing my hair. I wanted to look sexy, but I also wanted to make sure that my hair didn't start frizzing.

"A chair?" He frowned in confusion as he repeated what I'd told him to get.

"You speak English, yes?" I looked at him with a raised eyebrow and folded my arms across my chest. My heart was racing as I prepared myself mentally for what I was going to do next.

"Yes, ma'am. I'll get you a chair." He threw his shirt to

the ground and stood there in front of me with a chest of muscle and steel.

"Stat!" I barked.

"What are you, a dominatrix?" he asked me with a grin as he walked away. I didn't respond to his comments. In all honesty, I had no idea what I was doing and was making it up on the spot. He walked back with the chair and looked at me with a questioning face. "Where would you like me to put it?"

"Right next to me."

He placed the chair next to me and grinned. "What's next? A lap dance?" he asked me softly, and I could see the excitement in his eyes as he took a seat on the chair.

"Did I say you could sit there?" I frowned as I grabbed his arm and pulled him up.

"No, but I . . ."

"You what?" I smiled at him as his voice trailed off. His eyes were concentrated on my fingers that were lightly squeezing his cock through his briefs.

"Strip tease. Lap dance. You on chair." He groaned as I tugged on his cock slightly. "I mean me on chair with you rubbing up and down." He grabbed my arm as I pulled away from his cock. "Don't stop," he groaned as he looked at me.

"I'll stop if I want." I smiled and looked back at him. "Now get on your knees."

"Shouldn't I be the one saying that?" He laughed and then knelt down as I stared at him, unspeaking. "I've never seen this side of you before. I like a dominant Bianca."

"Don't tell me you thought I was shy and passive, like some sort of English rose?"

"I don't think anyone has made that mistake before, have they?" He laughed up at me, his eyes sparkling. "You're way too prickly to be a rose, though I suppose they do have thorns, don't they?"

"You're not making this easier on yourself," I said with a smile, and knelt down next to him. "Lie back. Flat on the ground," I said seductively as I straddled him.

"So I am getting a lap dance?" He lay flat on his back and he groaned as I moved back and forth on his hardness.

"Nope." I giggled as I leaned forward and grabbed his left hand and the other side of the handcuff. I quickly placed the cuff around the leg of the coffee table and jumped up. "Not right now, big boy."

"What are you doing?" He looked disappointed as he stared up at me, and I watched as he tried to move his left arm. "You're not going to leave me handcuffed to my coffee table, are you?"

"Not forever." I laughed.

"Bianca." He frowned, more agitated now.

"Don't you trust me, Jakob?" I teased him.

"Where are you going?" Jakob's voice was throaty, and I almost laughed at the despair in his tone.

"I'm just going to sit down." I grinned at him as I sat down in the chair he'd brought into the room.

"I wish you'd sit on me."

"I'm sure you do."

"You could even sit on my face, if you wanted to." He licked his lips slowly and deliberately. "That would be a nice treat for both of us."

"Yes, it would be, but it's not going to happen." I settled myself back on the chair and smoothed my skirt across my thighs.

"What are you doing?" Jakob's eyes narrowed as he watched me crossing my legs.

"Tell me if you recognize these lines," I said softly, and looked him in the eyes. I took a deep breath to calm my nerves and then started talking. "What's your new book about?" I said in a deep voice, channeling my inner Michael Douglas. Jakob's expression became extremely confused, and I knew he had no idea what I was doing, but that didn't stop me from continuing. I was imagining myself as Sharon Stone: sexy, confident, and very much in charge. "A detective. He falls for the wrong woman," I said sexily, letting myself completely assume the role of the extremely sexual and confident femme fatale.

"Uhm, Bianca." Jakob started laughing. "I have no idea what you're talking about. Is this your way of telling me that you have multiple personality disorder?"

"What?" I giggled and then did the only thing I could think of next. I lifted my right leg off my knee and spread my legs wide so that Jakob could see I had no underwear on.

"Oh," he said huskily as he swallowed. I could see him trying to move his arm away from the table. "*Basic Instinct.*"

"Of course you know it now," I said, and licked my lips slowly.

"Do it again?"

"What? The lines?" I said, feigning ignorance as to what he was asking me.

"No." He shook his head and groaned, his eyes never leaving my crotch area. "Flash me."

"Flash you?" I asked softly as I sat there and tapped my fingers against my leg. "Is that a command?"

"It's whatever you want it to be, baby."

"I think I'm the one in charge here." I stood up. "Don't you?"

"Bianca?" Jakob sounded confused as I left the room, and I grinned as I walked into his bedroom and opened his closet. I needed a blindfold, and I didn't have any of my scarves with me. I looked through his clothes and saw some ties, but they all looked too thin. I grinned as I saw a neat stack of scarves in the top-right corner of his closet. I grabbed a woolly black scarf and hurried back to the room where Jakob was staring at me woefully.

"You didn't think I was going to leave you tied up to the table, did you?" I teased him. "Who doesn't trust who now?"

"That wasn't my worry." He grinned. "I was scared you were going to leave me here with my hard-on and no release."

"Well I can't do that, can I?" I laughed and kneeled down next to him. "I'm going to blindfold you, okay?"

"A blindfold?" he asked, his smile growing wider.

"I'm a kinky bitch, what can I say?"

"If I called you a kinky bitch, you'd slap me." He laughed. "So right now, I'm just going to go with the flow."

"That always works." I knotted the scarf so that it wouldn't slide down his face and stood back and admired my handiwork.

"Jakob, what are you doing?" I stared at him as he wiggled his nose against the soft material of the blindfold.

"Remember when we were on the island?" he asked softly. "You told me to wiggle my nose to get the blindfold off."

"Oh, yeah." I laughed. "I forgot about that."

"I never forgot," he said softly. "I've wondered many times how you knew so much about blindfolds."

"Really, Jakob?" I laughed and pushed him back to the ground, before slowly sitting on his lap. I moved back and forth on his hardness and grinned in satisfaction as he groaned.

"I just wonder if you're not telling me something," he muttered as one of his hands grabbed my hip.

"You mean, like I'm a secret dominatrix?" I said as I leaned forward and pinched his nipples.

"Ow," he grunted, but he didn't tell me to stop. "Is that your confirmation?"

"You wish." I laughed.

"I don't know that I wish that," he said smoothly, his voice seducing me, even though I was the one in charge. "But I was wondering if you have a secret kinky side."

"Hmm." I leaned forward and sucked on his right nipple, gently tugging on it. "Maybe I do. And maybe it's not really a secret."

"Bianca," he groaned, and I heard the rattling of the handcuffs as he tried to move his other arm.

"Yes, Jakob?"

"You're killing me." He groaned.

"I'm sorry," I said, feeling anything but sorry, and moved up to kiss his lips. "And I know about blindfolds because I'm a bit of a sexual expert," I said against his lips. "I once wrote an article for *Playboy* about the ten sexiest movies ever made, and I had to watch a lot of almost-porn."

"You just get sexier." He sucked on my lower lip. "Anytime you want to write another article for *Playboy*, just let me know. Shit, even better if it's for *Hustler*." He groaned.

"You wish. And *Playboy* didn't even publish the article." I laughed and shook my head. "I ended up publishing it myself on a movie blog and got over ten thousand views. A lot of college guys were posting the link to the article on Facebook because they loved this one clip I showed from this seriously sexy French film. It made me more than a thousand dollars." I smiled as I remembered how happy I'd been that month.

"French films are deliciously risqué. The French are not ashamed of their bodies or sex," Jakob said.

"I know. The movie was so hot." I laughed and ran my hands along his jawline. "It was about this girl that was sleeping with her best friend's dad while she was actually dating the brother."

"Whoa, what?" he said, his voice shocked.

"She was dating the best friend's brother and then started

hooking up with the best friend's dad, who was also into candle play and spanking. And he brought her into his secret world of sex clubs and swapping and stuff."

"Sounds kinky."

"Oh, it was," I said softly, and ran my fingers across my breasts.

"Maybe we can watch it together sometime."

"Maybe." I laughed and then groaned. "I'm never going to write for the *New York Times*, am I? Not while reviewing almost-porn movies about girls hooking up with their best friend's dad."

"You can be whatever you want to be, Bianca London," he said, his voice suddenly serious. "And trust me, most art house movies are porn in disguise, so you're well on your way to the top."

"Right now, there's only one thing I want to be on top of. And that is you."

"Right now, all I want is for you to be the woman riding me. I'm ready for a gallop." He moved beneath me. "I'm ready to go all night long."

"You're always ready to go all night long," I said, and repositioned myself on top of him, his hardness planted firmly between my legs.

"Yeah, you can be the rider tonight, and maybe tomorrow I can be the cowboy."

"Cowboy?"

"I'm good with ropes, remember?" He smiled up at me.

"I wouldn't mind showing you some of my tricks to thank you for your riding lesson tonight."

"Tomorrow is the masquerade ball," I said out of nowhere. "I can't believe it is here already. I'm a little scared of what's going to happen."

"It's the annual Bradley Ball." Jakob shrugged, though his eyes never left my face. "It's innocent enough. I'm surprised that you agreed to go."

"Steve and Rosie want us to go. They want me to meet someone. I told them I'm not going anywhere without you." I stared at him intensely. "You know I wouldn't go without you, right? You know that I trust you implicitly, no matter how stupid my actions may be sometimes. I trust you with my life."

His hands stilled on my hips, and his expression grew cold. "I don't want to hear you saying things like that. Your life is not in danger."

"It felt like it was when I was with Rosie and Steve," I said quietly, still remembering the dread that had filled me.

"And you're just now telling me this?" he said angrily.

"I didn't know how to bring it up." I made a move to undo his blindfold, and he grunted.

"Not yet." He shook his head. "Fuck me first, and then we'll talk."

"Who do you think you are, telling me what to do?"

"I think I'm the guy that's driving you crazy. I think I'm the guy that needs to feel you rocking your hips back and forth as you bounce up and down on my hard cock like some sexy cowgirl. I think you're the girl that's going to scream out as you orgasm in ecstasy."

"You really have this sexy talk down, don't you?" I groaned as I got back onto his lap and rubbed myself on his hardness.

"You have the sexy moves and I have the sexy talk." He grunted. "I told you we were a perfect match." His voice was raspy, and I could feel his body tensing as I reached down and positioned his cock between my legs. I started moving back and forth so that the tip of his cock was rubbing my clit and I could feel my juices wetting him. "You're so sexy, Bianca." He groaned, and I looked down at his blindfolded face with a smile on my face. His jawline looked chiseled, and he was sporting an afternoon shadow. I reached down and ran my fingers across the soft bristles on his jaw and then leaned down and kissed him on the lips hard. I moved back slowly and I felt his cock inching inside of me at the same time that I pushed my tongue into his mouth. I brushed my breasts back and forth on his chest, enjoying the feel of his chest hair against my nipples. I moved my body up and brushed my nipples across his lips, and I laughed as he tried to lick and suck on them. However, I moved back down quickly, and he groaned.

"You're a tease." He groaned as his cock slipped out of me, and I continued moving back and forth on him. I was driving us both crazy with my moves.

"No such thing as a tease that gives you what you want,"

I said, and moved back on him roughly, grabbing his hardness and guiding him inside of me, before I started moving up and down on him in a rotating motion. I could hear Jakob breathing deeply beneath me, and he started moving his hips in a circular motion in time with my body. I could see the vein in his throat pulsating, and his hands were clenched as he climbed the mountain with me.

"Don't stop," he muttered as I slowed my movements, and I heard the clinking of metal against the table as he tried to move his hand. "Bianca, undo the handcuff."

"Why?" I said throatily, my vision blurring as my orgasm was reaching breaking point. I increased my speed again, and I felt the length of his cock sliding in and out of me smoothly.

"Because I want to hold on to you so that you don't ever stop whatever you're doing now," he said, his voice gruff and hoarse, as if he were having trouble keeping control. "Bianca," he groaned, and the sound of his voice took me over the edge.

"Jakob!" I screamed. I thrust my hips back and forth as I came diving off the mountain and into the cool calm sea below. "Jakob," I screamed again as I rotated my hips on top of him, and I felt him explode. Leaning forward I rubbed my breasts against his chest as I climaxed on top of him.

"That's my name," he said smugly a few seconds later, and when I looked up at his face, his bright blue eyes were gazing at me with love and desire.

"You got it off."

"You taught me well," he said with a wink, and I laughed as I leaned up and kissed him hard.

"I'm glad you acknowledge my prowess," I said as I removed the blindfold from his face completely and caressed his cheeks. "It's time you realized who holds the power in this relationship."

"You hold the power?" He grinned up at me and I could tell he was trying to stop laughing.

"Don't I?" I pushed my finger into his mouth, and he sucked on it eagerly.

"Do you?" he said with a smirk, and he yanked his arm hard. The next thing I knew, his hand was on my hip.

"What?" I stared down at him, gaping. "How did you get out of the handcuff?"

"This isn't my first time at the rodeo." He winked again, and I frowned as I made to get up off him. He grabbed my waist and rolled me over so that I was on the floor and he was on top. "I don't mean being tied up to a table with a sexy naked woman on top of me," he said as he pinned my arms to the floor and smirked down at me.

"Then what rodeo are you talking about?" I said sulkily, not wanting to think of him with another woman.

"Don't worry about it," he said, and leaned down and kissed my lips. "It doesn't even matter. The only thing that matters is you and me and how you make me feel like the most powerful man in the world."

"Really?"

"If I can make you scream and come like that, then hell yeah." He kissed down my neck. "You make me feel like Bassanio."

"Bassanio?"

"From *The Merchant of Venice*." He gazed down at me adoringly. "You're the Portia to my Bassanio."

"You want a pound of my flesh?" I raised an eyebrow, and he laughed.

"That was Shylock."

"He wasn't shy if he wanted flesh." I giggled, and Jakob shook his head. "And wait," I said with a frown. "Wasn't he the one that borrowed the money?"

"I'm not saying I'm exactly like Bassanio. I'm like him in the way that we both got the girl. The prettiest, most beautiful girl in all of the world."

"Jakob," I said, and rolled my eyes, but I couldn't stop myself from blushing. "Stop."

"I don't want to," he said, but he jumped up. "I really don't want to. I want to lie here with you all day and night, but there is a pounding in the back of my head that is telling me that we can't do that. Not yet. Not until we get to the bottom of this shit."

"Yeah." I sighed as I came back to earth. "I guess I should contact Blake and see what's going on."

"Yes, call him." Jakob stretched as he stood up. "I'm going to go and have a shower."

"Okay."

"You're welcome to join me if you want." He grinned, and I shook my head. I knew exactly what would happen if I joined him in the shower. And as much as I wanted it to happen, my mind was already back on the events from earlier in the day. I was already thinking about Rosie and Steve and their wanting us to attend the ball. I was once again wondering what Blake had to tell me. And my heart started racing as I thought about the possibility of Jeremiah still being alive.

~♥~

"Blake is on his way over." I pushed open the bathroom door and watched Jakob brushing his teeth naked. I stared at his bare butt and grinned as I walked up to him and squeezed his right butt cheek.

"Hey." Jakob spat out the toothpaste in his mouth as he jumped slightly. "What're you doing?"

"Just feeling my man's buns of steel."

"Are you calling me Superman?"

"Maybe. You're pretty super in the bed."

"That's what I like to hear," Jakob growled, and turned around and swept me into his arms. "I'm super in the bathroom as well."

"Did you not hear me just now?" I giggled as I felt his manhood brush up against me. "Blake is on his way over."

"Hey, I can go fast as well. I'm good at sprints and marathons."

"I'm sure you are." I wrapped my arms around his neck

and kissed him softly. "However, we don't have time for either at this point."

"Not even five minutes?"

"Five minutes isn't enough to satisfy me."

"It's enough to satisfy me." He winked, and I laughed.

"I thought you'd already been satisfied?" I reached down and grabbed his already hard cock and tugged on it gently. He groaned and reached down and grabbed my hand.

"Don't start something you're not going to finish," he grunted against my lips.

"Who says I'm not going to finish?" I kissed him hard, and I felt his tongue entering my mouth, forceful and minty. His tongue played with mine, and I sucked on it eagerly, momentarily forgetting my nerves at what Blake was going to tell me.

"Oh, you're going to finish."

"Oh, you're certain of that?"

"Yes." He nodded, and his hands reached down and up under my shirt. His fingers dug into my skin as they made their way up to my breasts. "I am pretty certain of that." He grinned at me as his fingers reached my nipples, and he ran the palms of his hands across them before pinching them softly.

"Oh, Jakob." I moaned as he pulled my T-shirt off and threw it to the ground. He leaned down and took my right nipple in his mouth and sucked on it gently before grabbing me around the waist and pulling me into him. My breasts crushed against his chest, and he leaned down and kissed me again. We stood there just kissing, and I could feel the stirrings of desire as his cock rubbed against my belly.

"On your knees," he said as he pulled away from me.

"What?" I looked at him in surprise, and he pointed to the floor.

"On your knees," he said again. This time his voice was stronger and more authoritative.

"On my knees?"

"Now." He stared at me, and I watched as his lip twitched slightly. "You were in charge a few minutes ago, and now it's my turn."

"I didn't know we were taking turns." I smirked.

"On your knees." He leaned over and pinched my right nipple, and I squealed slightly as my panties grew wet. I licked my lips slowly and sank to my knees. My breath caught as I stared up into his bright blue eyes.

"What now?"

"Make me come," he said, and leaned back against the sink, his hard cock flopping around in front of me.

"Make you come?" I swallowed hard at the tone in his voice. I never knew a voice could turn me on so much.

"And swallow." He grabbed my hair and tilted my head up. "I don't want to have to shower again."

"Or what?" I said lightly as my tongue darted out of my mouth and licked the length of his shaft. Jakob's breath caught and he pulled my hair harder.

"Do you want to find out?" he asked huskily. Instead

of answering, I got to work, taking the tip of him into my mouth and sucking gently, enjoying the clean taste of him. I felt powerful as he hardened even more, and I took him as deep as I could without gagging. I wasn't sure how some women were able to swallow a man's whole cock, especially someone of Jakob's size. He wasn't enormous, but he had certainly been blessed. I shifted my legs as I felt myself growing wetter. I wanted him again. Inside me: deep, hard, loving, and dominating. I wanted to feel the length of his sex as his body ground on top of mine. I started moving my mouth back and forth on him even faster. Jakob pulled my hair, and the pain turned me on even more. I was still bobbing my head up and down when the sound of my phone ringing finally hit my brain.

"Shit." Jakob groaned as I jumped up and grabbed my T-shirt.

"That must be Blake."

"Fuck it." He sighed, and I looked down and giggled. His cock was standing at attention, and I knew he was close to blowing his load.

"I have to go and get the door." I leaned over and kissed him on the cheek.

"You're not answering the door like that." His face was dark as he growled. "You don't have a bra on, and that T-shirt is barely covering your thong."

"I'll pull on some shorts." I rolled my eyes.

"You're not answering the door like that," he said firmly as his hands cupped my breasts through my T-shirt. "Those are mine and only mine. I don't want some other guy getting a view of the nipples that I made hard."

"Jakob, you're being ridiculous. You know Blake is just a friend."

"A friend that wanted you and most probably still wants you," he said grumpily as the doorbell rang.

"Jakob, stop being stupid."

"Put on a bra and some shorts," he said as he grabbed a pair of black sweatpants. "I'm going to answer the door."

"Without a shirt on?" I said snarkily.

"And with no boxers either." He grinned as he walked to the door. "Maybe he'll notice that he interrupted us at an inopportune moment."

"You're gross."

"Nope. Just horny." He laughed and slapped me on the bottom as he hurried out of the room. "I expect you to finish what you started when he leaves."

"You're the one who started it," I protested as my face flushed, but he just walked out of the room.

~𝒪

"Sorry about earlier, Bianca." Blake's face was flushed, and he looked up at me with a guilty expression. "I hope you weren't waiting at the coffee shop too long."

"It's fine. I was more worried about you," I said as I sat next to him. I could see Jakob glaring at me as I rubbed Blake's leg.

"I got caught up at the library." Blake's eyes were blazing

with excitement. "I didn't want to leave until I was clear about what I found."

"What exactly did you find?" Jakob asked impatiently. "Is my dad alive?"

"Well, I'm not sure." Blake leaned forward as his voice lowered. "But there is no death certificate for him."

"What do you mean there is no death certificate?" Jakob frowned. "There has to be a death certificate."

"There isn't one that I can find." Blake shook his head. "Which isn't altogether unusual, because they never found a body."

"Yes, we know that." Jakob rolled his eyes.

"Did you know that your dad was working on a cryo-preservation machine?"

"A what?" I said in confusion.

"A machine to help humans stay alive forever."

"Like in *Vanilla Sky*?" My jaw dropped, and I looked at Jakob. "That's a movie with Tom Cruise and Penélope Cruz."

"Ask me if I care." Jakob smiled at me. "Though I'm glad to know if I ever need a movie-related lifeline, I can call you."

I stuck my tongue out at him and turned to Blake. "So what you're saying is that Jeremiah is alive and will live forever?"

"No." Blake laughed. "I don't know that. As far as I can see, there are no machines that can guarantee an everlasting life. No one can live forever."

"So he's dead, then?"

"I don't know. We have no valid proof of his death."
Blake shook his head, and Jakob jumped up, an exasperated
look on his face.

"So what are you saying?" Jakob sounded annoyed.
"Aside from the fact that my dad may be dead or alive? Is that
what you were so excited to tell us?"

"No." Blake grinned and gave me a look as if to say, *Is he
always like this?*

"So you know how when you and Bianca came back and
they arrested him for embezzling, it came out that Larry
Maxwell became Larry Renee?"

"Yes, we knew that already."

"And you know how Rosie is Larry's daughter?"

"Yup." Jakob was irritated, and I gave him a short look.
I wondered if his blue balls were why he was being such a
dickhead. Maybe I needed to take him into the bedroom and
finish the job I'd started before we talked to Blake.

"Well, did you also know that Larry has only been married once?"

"What?" I frowned, and Jakob stopped pacing back and
forth.

"Larry has only been married once," Blake said with a
grin. "And that was to Rosie's mother, Brigitta."

"But what about Mrs. Renee?" I said with a frown. "I've
met her. We've both met her." I looked at Jakob, and Jakob
nodded his assent.

"Yeah, we both met her."

"What if I told you that Mrs. Renee didn't exist?"

"We saw her in the flesh," Jakob said. "Unless you're now going to tell us that the frightened woman we saw was a ghost." His voice was sarcastic as he stared at me. "There's another one for you, Bianca. Maybe we're real-life ghost whisperers."

"*Ghost Whisperer* was a TV show, not a movie." I rolled my eyes at him and then looked back at Blake. "But we did see her, Blake. She definitely existed."

"Yes, I believe you saw *someone*." Blake nodded. "However, whoever that someone was, was not Mrs. Renee. She was not related to Larry."

"But they've been married for years," I said, as my mind raced back. "I know that for sure. I've met her before."

"Maybe they were common-law spouses," Jakob said. "Is that all you've got for us?"

"Did you know that Larry bought the house in Long Island the week after Oliver Case died?"

"Oliver Case?" Jakob frowned. "Steve's dad?"

"Yes. Oliver Case had one relative at the time of his death, a younger sister by the name of Penny. She was never married. And she disappeared a couple of days after her brother died."

"How do you know that?"

"I uncovered a missing persons report in my research. She left her job and never came back—her landlady filed a report a few days after the funeral. She said that Oliver was the one who sent in the rent check every month."

"Okay, so say all that is true," Jakob said as he sat back down. "Say Mrs. Renee was Oliver's sister. Why would she marry Larry? Or pretend to be Larry's wife?"

"That's what I wanted to know." Blake grinned excitedly. "Why would Oliver's sister disappear and take up with Larry?"

"What did you come up with?" I asked, and leaned in closer to Blake.

"Not much." He sighed, but then he smiled again. "But we can ask her."

"We don't even know where she is, and we also don't know if Mrs. Renee really is this Penny," Jakob snapped, obviously tiring of Blake's dramatics.

"Ah, but we do!" Blake grinned.

"How?"

"Look." He opened up his messenger bag and pulled out some sheets of paper. "Look at this." He handed them to me, and I looked at each one carefully. The first one was a copy of Penny Case's driver's license. There was a photo of a young woman, and my heart stopped for a second as I stared at the photo. I didn't even have to see the other papers to know that Penny was the woman we'd met as Mrs. Renee, but I looked them over anyway. I handed the papers to Jakob silently, my heart racing as I thought about what we now knew. Steve's aunt was married to Larry. Oliver Case—the man who had been taken advantage of by Jeremiah, Larry, and my father—had a sister. A sister who presumably loved him. And she'd married Larry. Or had gotten into some sort of relationship with Larry. I just didn't know why. She had to have known that Larry had been one of the guys who had taken advantage of her brother, didn't she?

"Okay, so Penny is Mrs. Renee." Jakob said, his voice surprised. "What else did you find out?"

"What would you do if I told you that you have a third sibling?" Blake said casually, and Jakob and I looked at each other in shock.

"What?" Jakob jumped up again. "What are you talking about?"

"You have a sibling." Blake nodded.

"I know my father didn't have any other kids." Jakob shook his head. "Are you saying my mother did?"

"I'm saying that your father has a love child." Blake shrugged. "I don't know what he told you."

"How do you know this?" Jakob said with a frown.

"Because there was a blackmail claim." Blake paused. "And your father paid a million dollars to keep it hush-hush."

"To whom?"

"Well, that's the question." Blake frowned. "I'm not sure."

"How do you know all of this?" Jakob said in a direct voice. "Unless you found some sort of signed declaration from my maybe dead and maybe alive father? And how is that connected to Penny?"

"We know that because Mrs. Renee's blackmail letter is now in the hands of Penny's ex-landlady."

"And you know this how?" Jakob said with a raised eyebrow.

"Because I spoke to her," Blake said with a grin. "She's still alive. She never told the police because she felt like they never did much after Penny disappeared. She was happy to tell me everything she could when I called and told her I was a history student doing some research."

"So then Penny sent the blackmail letter?" Jakob said matter-of-factly. "If Penny lived there and it was returned back to her address."

"This is where it gets good." Blake shook his head. "It was Penny's handwriting." He opened his bag again and pulled out another piece of paper. "This is what took me so long. I got the landlady to fax me a copy of the note. She didn't have a scanner to send it from home. I had to wait for her to go to a Staples, and then I had to go and find a store to give her a number to fax it to me." He scratched his head. "I wasn't about to risk having her fax it to my e-mail address."

"So you have the letter?" I asked eagerly, and he handed it to me.

I glanced at Jakob and began to read aloud.

" 'My Dearest Jeremiah, I can't keep it in any longer. You are the love of my life, and I am yours. I don't want to keep quiet. I don't want to do this alone. We've been through too much. Our love can change everything. We have a bond now. If you continue to shut me out, I will tell the world. I will tell them everything. We have a child that shares our DNA. I can accept yours if you can accept mine. Forever yours.'" I paused and turned the page over. "That's it, no name." I groaned and looked at Jakob to gauge his response. His eyes were narrowed, and I could tell he was thinking hard.

"So we know it is most probably from Penny, but what if it's not? It's likely from her, unless . . ." He paused and stared at me for a few seconds, his gaze darkening.

"Unless what?" I said, my throat constricting as I realized what he was trying to say. "No, it's not from my mom. It can't be, can it?" I gazed at Blake, my face red and hot.

"No, it's not your mom." Blake shook his head, and I let out a deep breath. "I admit, I did some research to check. However, it's not her."

"Thank God." I shuddered and then frowned. "So who else could it be? And who is Jeremiah's third child?"

"It's not Rosie, is it?" Jakob spoke up, and I stared at him in shock.

"You don't think it could be Rosie, surely?" I felt sick to my stomach. If Rosie was Jeremiah's child and she was dating David, well, that would just be sick. I didn't even want to think about it, no matter how much I now hated her.

"That would explain why she was trying so hard to help bring you down," Jakob said. "I've always thought she had to have some sort of secret agenda."

"But her dad is Larry, right?" I looked at Blake questioningly. "And she's dating David. Would she really date her own half brother?" I almost threw up at the thought.

"I don't think Rosie is Jeremiah's daughter," Blake said, and made a face. "Even though I can't stand her, I don't think she'd stoop to incest."

"So then who?" I said, and looked at Blake. "Who can it be?"

"We'll figure it out," Jakob said, and sat down next to me. "We'll figure it out together."

"Yeah, we'll get to the bottom of this." Blake nodded. "Now, what happened with you and Rosie and Steve?"

"They wanted me to go with them to meet someone." I spoke carefully. "They didn't say who, but I keep thinking that they were talking about Jeremiah. I think he might still be alive, but I don't know what he would want with me. Anyway, they want me and Jakob to go to the annual Bradley Masquerade Ball to meet this person."

"Do you think that's a good idea?" Blake frowned. "It sounds like a setup."

"I know, but what else can we do?" I sighed. "I didn't even know Rosie knew Steve. I'm just confused. I need to find out what's going on."

"There's one last thing we could do," Blake said, his eyes thoughtful.

"What's that?"

"I can go and see Larry," Blake said. "I can question him."

"Not alone," Jakob said with a small shake of the head. "We'll all go."

"But what is Larry going to do?" I pursed my lips. "I think that's a waste of time."

"Not if we tell him we know about Penny," Jakob said thoughtfully.

"But we don't know much," I protested.

"Then we have to find out more before the ball on Saturday," Jakob said, and Blake nodded. "We need to make sure that when we arrive at the ball, we're armed with as much information as possible."

"That's true." I chewed on my lower lip and stared at the two men next to me. I realized that I didn't feel anxious or worried. I felt calm. Frustrated and thoughtful, but my heart wasn't racing as it would have been when I first started this quest. I was no longer alone in this crazy adventure. I no longer felt like someone playing the role of a brave person—now I really was brave. And I had two men by my side who had my back. "So should we go now?"

"I don't think so." Blake laughed along with Jakob. "We have to figure out exactly where he is. I'll make some calls and we can all go tomorrow morning."

"Why don't we try to find Penny first?" Jakob suggested. "If we can get some concrete facts from her, then maybe we can approach Larry with someone real. Then maybe he can prepare us for what Steve and Rosie have planned."

"Or what he has planned." I sighed. "If Larry is the mastermind behind it all, he's not going to tell us what's going on."

"Yeah, but if he's the mastermind, there is something he wants," Jakob said. "And if my father is alive, then Larry is still number two."

"If your father is alive, then what does *he* want? Why pretend to be dead?"

"Heaven only knows." Jakob sighed.

"Heaven and Penny Case." Blake tapped his forehead. "Even if Mrs. Renee isn't Penny Case, she has a story."

Jakob stood there, a distant look in his eyes. "Why do I have the feeling that no matter what we find out, we're still going to be blindsided at the ball?"

∽

"My mother used to dream of being a famous writer," Jakob said as we got dressed to go out to dinner later that night. "She told me that when she was younger, she would write poems for everyone she met, but she knew her parents wouldn't approve of her trying to be an author."

"What were your grandparents like?"

"I don't know." He shook his head. "They died before I was born." He took out a crisp white shirt. "Sometimes I wonder what would have been different for my mother if she hadn't had to fend for herself from such a young age."

"I didn't know that."

He started to do up his shirt, and I watched as his fingers deftly handled the buttons. "Black or red?" He held up two ties to me.

"You have to wear a bow tie." I grinned. "A black one."

"Yes, ma'am." He winked at me. "What are you going to do to me if I don't?"

"Spank you." I winked back at him, and he laughed.

"Ooh, I think I'll wear a pink one, then." He turned around and bent forward. "I'll take my spanking now."

"You wish." I laughed. "So how did your mom meet Jeremiah?"

"She used to work in the cafeteria at Harvard," he said softly. "They had a relationship, and he ended up marrying someone with a name and money to match his family's."

"David's mom?"

"Yeah." He nodded.

"And she was okay with the fact that he already had a kid with another woman?"

"I don't think Macy Vanderbilt cared." His lips twisted scornfully. "My mom said she would have done anything to be with Jeremiah. In fact, she stole him from someone else."

"Oh?"

"Yeah, he was a player." Jakob shook his head. "Typical man, my mom always said."

"That's sad."

"I know." He sighed. "I wish she hadn't gotten involved with him. I just don't understand what she saw in him, why she loved him so much. When she died, I found a book full of poems, and most of them were about her love for him."

"That's so sad. He wasn't even worth it." I could feel tears coming to my eyes. "Why does the heart always fall for the wrong person?"

"It doesn't always." Jakob grabbed my hands and pulled me toward him. "Sometimes the heart falls for exactly the right person."

"Do you ever think about the fact that if it wasn't for all

of this, we wouldn't have met?" I said softly, and gazed up at him.

"All the time." He nodded and sighed. "And I don't know what to think about that. If it wasn't for my mother's heartbreak, I might never have found you."

"Maybe we would have found each other in a different way."

"Maybe."

"Do you think your dad is still alive?" I changed the subject as I thought about the night ahead of us. "Do you think he's the one pulling all the strings?"

"I don't know." Jakob sighed, and I could see that his eyes had hardened. "It wouldn't surprise me. For all intents and purposes, he died in a plane crash." He looked up at me. "But I wouldn't be shocked if he faked his death."

"Why would he do that?" I asked him softly, and he pulled me into his arms and held me close to his body. I could feel his heart racing as he stroked my hair.

"That's what we need to find out." He pursed his lips. "Something seems off though. Why would Steve and Rosie want you to meet my dad?"

"I don't know." I bit my lower lip. "And does David know? He would have to, right?"

"I don't know why they would keep it from him," Jakob said, looking thoughtful. "But yeah, I don't think that David knows anything. To be honest, I think Rosie's playing David."

"And she's being led by Larry?"

"Yeah." He looked at me with puzzled eyes. "But I don't know what Larry gets out of it."

"Money?"

"He has money." Jakob shook his head. "Unless my dad really is alive, and he's the one calling the shots."

"Larry seems like he would do anything for your dad."

"Yeah. I guess." He shrugged. "I guess we'll find out tonight."

"Yeah, I hope so." I suddenly thought of something and grabbed his hand. "Will you be okay if he's still alive?"

"It wouldn't matter either way to me." He shook his head, his eyes hardening. "Hold on, I want to read you one of my mom's poems before we leave."

"Okay." I watched as Jakob walked over to his nightstand and opened the top drawer and pulled out a leather-bound notepad. He flicked through the filled pages and then walked back toward me.

"'Silence. Silence is what I feel when I see him now. No birds are chirping. No sunshine is burning. No rain is pouring. The world is still. And I lay awake in all my glory. Waiting. Waiting for him to come back to me. Not even my heartbeat makes a sound. My eyes don't blink. I can't miss the second when he comes back to me. The second he is mine. The second that the silence stops. The silence is deafening.'" He closed the journal and looked up at me. "I read this, and I think of my mother. I think of her crying late at night when she thought I was asleep. I think of her sitting at the kitchen table every night writing, and I wonder how long she waited. How long she hoped. How long her heart ached . . . for *him*. I read this, and my hatred for Jeremiah Bradley grows. He's nothing to me but a blood donor."

"That's so sad." I put a hand on his arm. "How can one man cause so much pain?"

"She said he was kind." He looked at me thoughtfully and shook his head in disbelief. "She said he was the kindest man in the world."

"Jeremiah?" I looked at him in shock. "I'd never have thought Jeremiah Bradley was a kind man."

"Yeah, me either, but I can remember her clearly telling me. She told me that the man she loved was her first friend. The first person who was truly kind to her. He didn't care that she was poor or that she worked in a cafeteria. He was the first man to ever look her in the eyes and ask her if she'd had a good day. She said he was the first man who had seen her as a person." His voice broke. "And I hate Jeremiah for being that person. I hate him for making her fall in love with him. I hate him for ruining her life. I hate him for fooling her. He didn't love her. He just used her." Jakob's voice was angry, and he looked away from me. "How could she love him? How could she have spent so many years heartbroken?"

"I'm sorry." I stroked the side of his face. "I'm so sorry, Jakob."

"She wrote a poem about her heartbreak," he said. "I think it was that poem that really made me hate your parents, your mother especially."

"I see." I looked down, not sure what to say. I could em-
pathize with him. I felt for his mother as well, but I didn't
know how to accept his hatred of my mother. I didn't even
know how to feel myself. How could my mother have cheated
with Jeremiah Bradley? I didn't know why she would have
done that to my father.

"I'm sorry." He sighed. "I shouldn't have said that. I
don't blame them, Bianca. Not anymore. I don't know what
happened, but I don't blame them."

"Are we ever going to get over this, Jakob?" I sighed.

"Bianca, there's something I want to say to you." Jakob's
face was serious, and my stomach lurched. I wasn't sure how
much more I could take. What was he going to say? How was
he going to break my heart?

"Go on, then." I turned away from him, unable to look
in his eyes as I prepared for the worst. I wasn't even sure if
I'd have a heart after all of this. How many times could it be
broken and heal itself again? My father and Rosie had pushed
me to the limits, but Jakob had the power to stop my heart
from beating ever again.

"I know you might find this hard to believe," he said
softly. "You matter to me more than anything in the world.
Your love, your heart, your safety, your happiness is what
I live for now. My mother was my whole world, and her
memory has guided me all these years, but all that is second-
ary to what I feel for you. My mother will always live on in
my heart, but she's not the one guiding my life anymore.
She's not the one I think of late at night." He grabbed my

hands and squeezed. "You're my number one priority, Bianca, and I don't care what happened in the past. I don't care what happened with our parents. Whatever we find out next, it won't change anything. It won't stop how much I love you."

"I just don't know why my mother would have—"

"Stop." He put his fingers against my lips. "We don't know what happened. Until we know, let's not guess."

"If I see your father at the ball, I'm going to . . ." My voice trailed off, and I sighed. "I don't know what I'm going to do."

"Have you spoken to Blake?"

"He said he's going to come over so we can all chat before we leave." I held up my black dress with the delicate black feathers running down the side to match my mask. "Do you think this is okay? Will I look like the Black Swan?"

"It's sexy." He stared at the dress in my hand and touched the fabric lightly. I glanced up at him in his suit and my stomach flipped at the sexiness he exuded. "Soft and silky with a high slit, what are you thinking will happen at the ball, Ms. Swan?"

"What do you mean, Louis the Fourteenth?" I teased him as I ran my fingers down his long regal jacket. Jakob had agreed to try on our outfits early to check the fit, so that on the night of the ball, we weren't rushing around to fix anything. And if it meant I got to see him in his sexy king getup, so much the better.

"I mean are you hoping to get lucky while we dance the night away?"

"Jakob, tonight we can have fun." I poked him in the chest. "But on the night of the ball, we have to be serious. That means we will be focused. There will be no getting lucky while we are working. We have to have all of our wits about us and concentrate."

"That doesn't mean we can't have some fun as well." He grabbed my fingers and brought them down his chest to his crotch, so that I could feel his hardness pulsating beneath my fingers.

"What fun do you think we're going to have?" I said breathlessly.

"Don't wear any panties, Sharon Stone, and you'll find out."

"You're never going to forget that, are you?"

"You got that right. Even when we're old and gray with grandkids, I'll be joking around about how I married the second coming of Sharon Stone. No pun intended."

"You better not." I laughed, but my insides warmed as he talked about us with grandkids.

"You owe me." He grinned. "Wear no panties to dinner tonight, then I won't expect that on the night of the ball."

"I guess you'll see what I decide when we get to the restaurant," I said, licking my lips slowly.

"You tease." He grinned as he started to take off his costume. "Thank God I don't have to wear this getup every day."

"Hmmm," I said as I stared at his bare chest and grinned. I walked over and ran my fingers down his abs. "What time is our reservation again? There's something we need to do before we go," I whispered as I dropped to my knees and started to unbutton his Louis XIV breeches. Jakob groaned as I pulled the pants down and I grinned up at him, feeling a surge of power before I took him into my mouth. The night of the ball would be serious, but that didn't mean we couldn't have fun tonight.

seven

Nicholas London
Decades Ago

As much as things change, they stay the same. Love, jealousy, and hate all make the world go round.

"I'm going up to see Jeremiah," I told Andy, the doorman. He nodded and waved me toward the elevators without signing me in. He always let me go up without signing in, even though the protocol of the building required it. But Andy had known me for years. He'd known me when I'd been Jeremiah's friend, he'd known me when I'd been Jeremiah's business partner, and he knew me now that I was just an employee. And he'd never treated me differently. I liked that about Andy.

I pushed the button for the penthouse, and as the elevator doors slid closed I thought of Bianca, my beautiful daughter. She was only a small child, but she was so intelligent, and her wide hazel eyes were wise beyond her years. My heart was filled with joy and a nervous sort of angst as I rode up to see Jeremiah. I knew I was doing the right thing, yet it didn't feel good. I wasn't sure how he'd react to what I had to tell him. I'd have to find a way to make sure Bianca was well taken care of. She was the one who would suffer if things went wrong.

I smiled as I thought of my daughter. Angelina and I had wanted kids so very badly. And even now, when things were so tense, Bianca could still bring us together. She was our lifeline to the future. I rubbed my temple gently as I felt a headache setting in. Life was so complicated now, so full of mistakes and regrets. Sometimes I wished I could get back to the beginning. Sometimes I wished that I'd never gone to Harvard, but then I realized that I never would have met Angelina, and I knew that I wouldn't change a thing.

The elevator ride seemed excruciatingly long, and when I finally arrived at the penthouse, I felt surprisingly calm. I held my head high and called out for Jeremiah.

"Jeremiah, it's me, Nick. Where are you?" I headed for the living room, but it was empty. The whole apartment was oddly quiet, and I supposed Macy must have taken David out shopping somewhere. I was glad she wasn't home. We still didn't get along, and I knew she blamed me for the fact that Jeremiah had an illegitimate son with Joanie. After all, I was Joanie's friend. I was the one who had introduced her to the group. I wished now that I hadn't. It had ruined her life— but then, the group had ruined so many lives. I was lucky to be left unscathed. I heard a faint noise coming from the bedroom, and I walked toward it slowly, hoping that Jeremiah wasn't occupied with a prostitute, as was his penchant when he was stressed.

"I love you, Jeremiah." The familiar voice sounded soft and begging. "I won't let you discard me again. I've done everything you've ever asked of me." I froze as I peeked into the room and saw the couple on the bed.

Jeremiah looked down at his companion and my hand flew to my mouth as I watched them embrace. I let out a loud gasp, and they both looked up at me in shock.

"I didn't want you to find out this way—" Jeremiah grimaced, but I had nothing to say. I turned around and ran back to the elevator, furious at his betrayal. As I stood in the elevator my head pounded, and I knew nothing would be able to dull it. I hurried out of the building with one thought in my mind: Nothing was going to be the same again. Absolutely nothing.

eight

Bianca London

Present Day

"I have good news and bad news," Blake said as he walked into Jakob's apartment early the next morning.

"What's the good news?" I asked as I dried my wet hair with a towel. I noticed Blake looking me over quickly, and I was glad that Jakob wasn't there to witness Blake's keen assessment of my body. I stifled a yawn as I looked over at him. I didn't want to have to blush my way through an excuse that concealed the fact that Jakob and I had had sex in the restaurant bathroom during our dinner and then all over his apartment when we'd gotten home. I thought the adrenaline and excitement was giving us more energy, which I suppose was better than letting fear of the unknown take us over.

"I found Penny Case." His eyes lit up as he spoke, and I smiled at the eagerness in his voice.

"Jakob, Blake's here!" I shouted through to the bedroom. "And he's found Penny Case."

"I'm coming." Jakob walked out of the bedroom, drops of water still glistening on his naked chest. He was wearing a pair of red plaid boxers, and my mouth watered as I stared at him.

Blake looked at Jakob and then back at me, and I could see disappointment in his eyes as it clicked that Jakob and I had likely showered together.

"Hi, Blake." Jakob nodded as he came and stood next to me, his hand casually cupping my ass as he kissed my cheek.

"I found Penny Case." Blake shifted uncomfortably as Jakob continued to touch me possessively.

"Would you like coffee, Blake?" I moved away from Jakob.

"No, thanks." He shook his head.

"So what's the bad news, then?"

"She's flying out of JFK this afternoon." Blake frowned. "She's taking a flight to Paris."

"Why's that bad news?" Jakob looked puzzled.

"Well, we don't know where she is right now," Blake said. "And then she'll be at the airport, and we won't have a way to talk to her because we're not flying anywhere." He sighed. "I guess we can wait around the terminal in hopes of seeing her."

"I have a better idea," Jakob said with a smile. "We'll get three tickets on the same flight, or another one if that is full."

"I can't afford that," Blake said, his voice low.

"Well, I can." Jakob grinned. "It's times like this that I enjoy being rich."

"Show-off." I rolled my eyes at him, but I shared his excitement. "It's times like this that I enjoy you being rich as well."

"And you don't care the other times?"

"Nope. In fact, I wish you weren't so rich. You wouldn't have so many different women after you, and you wouldn't have all these people after your money."

"And to think I used to think you were a gold digger," Jakob said, and then laughed as I glared at him.

"Whatever." I turned around and smiled at Blake. "So we'll go to the airport and wait by her terminal. You know what flight she's traveling on, right?"

"Yup." He nodded. "Thanks to the Internet and frequent-flier miles."

"What?" I frowned as I gazed at him.

"She upgraded her ticket to first class." Blake's smile was wide as he spoke, expressing his approval. "I spotted her on a forum asking how to convert the points from her credit card."

"How did you know it was her?"

"She's old-school." Blake said, his voice deep and thoughtful. "Her username was Pennycase1."

"And you're sure it's the same person?" Jakob asked with a frown. "Would she really be so dumb as to use her real name?"

"I'm pretty confident it's her." Blake nodded. "I looked at her profile to see the e-mail address she was using on the off chance that it wasn't private, and it wasn't. I then searched online to see if that e-mail address was being used on any other accounts online, and lo and behold, it was."

"Oh?" I asked eagerly. "Carry on."

"It was registered to a weight-loss group," he said, "and a grief group."

"A support group?" Jakob asked, suddenly more interested in the conversation.

"Yes, it turns out Penny Case lost a brother many years ago. She wanted advice on how to handle the pain she still feels for her brother Oliver."

"Oliver Case." I gasped and looked at Jakob. "It has to be her."

"And get this . . ." Blake paused for dramatic effect.

"What?" I said, my heart racing.

"She was on one other site." He paused again, and I could see that Jakob was getting irritated.

"Come on, Blake."

"It was a site about relationships," Blake continued. "Taboo relationships."

"What sort of taboo?" Jakob asked with a frown.

"Well, most of the people were former mistresses now worried that their new husbands were going to cheat." Blake scratched the side of his face. "To be honest, I don't know why she was on the site. She never answered or asked any questions."

"So that really wasn't helpful." Jakob shook his head.

"Well, it was, kinda," I said with an encouraging smile to

Blake. "We know that Penny has some sort of connection to a taboo relationship, and we know that she was never legally married to Larry. So maybe there is a reason why, a deeper darker reason than we know about."

"That's a very tenuous connection to make, but I suppose it could be true," Jakob said. He grabbed his phone from the table and quickly made a call. "Lucy, put me through to travel, please." He looked at me as he spoke, and his eyes pierced mine with a fiery look as we stood there staring at each other. "Hi, Jason, this is Jakob. I need you to book three flights for me. Flying out of JFK today. Hold on." He looked at Blake. "What's the flight number?"

"AF250," Blake said without a blink, and I smiled.

"I can't believe you remember that."

"That was easy." He laughed. "I grew up in the South; all my uncles drove Ford F-250s."

"Oh, ha-ha." I laughed and then turned to Jakob, who was back to frowning again.

"Air France flight 250," he barked into the phone. "Tickets for me, Bianca London, and Blake Matthews." Jakob grunted at something Jason said on the phone. "Then get me first-class tickets!" he shouted. "I don't care about the cost. No, I do not need you to check to see if there is a cheaper flight on another airline. Just book it." He paused for a few seconds and then smiled. "Good. No, there's no need. I'll take care of the rest. Thanks, Jason," he said, and hung up. "Done. We're booked for the same flight. Now let's all pack some suitcases."

"Suitcases?" I frowned. "Are we actually getting on the flight?"

"No, of course not." Jakob shook his head.

"Then why . . ." My voice trailed off as I saw Jakob smirking.

"TSA will think we're suspicious," Blake spoke up, and looked at Jakob with newfound respect. "Good thinking."

"Thanks. Come through." Jakob started walking toward the bedroom and turned to Blake. "Feel free to pack my clothes into a bag." He handed him a small Louis Vuitton suitcase and then turned to me. "Now, I'm afraid I don't have many women's clothes for you to pack."

"Trying to reassure me you're not a cross-dresser?" I said with a smirk.

"No, what I'm saying is I haven't fucked any women here." He tilted his head. "So none of them have left their clothes."

I gasped at his comment, my face reddening at his words, and I could see Blake looking away with widened eyes.

"You're a jerk," I muttered as I glared at him. Jakob just smiled.

"Doesn't that make you feel better to know you're the only one who's been here? You're the only one I've fucked in the bed, in the shower, on the couch, in the kitchen, on the new sheepskin rug . . ."

"We haven't had sex on the rug." I frowned.

"Not yet, we haven't." Jakob licked his lips, and my stomach stirred.

"You're so inappropriate. We have a guest."

"I'm sure Blake doesn't mind," Jakob said lightly. "He knows what couples do."

"I don't mind," Blake said, his voice slightly squeaky, and I felt bad about him having to witness this. I loved him madly, but Jakob could be a jerk sometimes. When this was all over, we would have to have a talk about considering other people's feelings.

"So what do you want me to pack?" I changed the subject, not wanting to get into an argument at that moment.

"Some sexy thongs and . . ." Jakob's voice trailed off as I pinched him hard. "Just pack some T-shirts," he said finally. "I'm sure they won't be going through the suitcases, but we don't want to arouse suspicion by traveling with no luggage or empty bags."

"Fine," I said, and all of a sudden I got very nervous and excited. "What are we going to ask Penny when we get there?" I said quietly, and both men turned to me with blank expressions.

"That's the million-dollar question," Jakob said with a sigh. "If we knew what to ask and how to ask it, we'd be so much closer to the truth."

"Plus she'll recognize us." I made a face. "What if she sees us and makes a run for it?"

"We'll wait in the restroom until Blake lets us know he's spotted her. Then we ambush her."

"I hope we're not going to kidnap her as well," Blake said jokingly, but Jakob didn't laugh.

"Focus, guys," Jakob said as if he hadn't just been acting like the biggest asshole in the world. "We need Penny to get us access to Larry, and we need Larry to figure out what's going down at the ball. And we need to know what's going down at the ball so that we don't find ourselves in some sort of crazy predicament."

"Like waking up on a deserted island with a stranger?" I said innocently.

"No, like waking up on a deserted island with a crazy, movie-obsessed woman."

"You're the one who took me there." I poked him in the chest.

"And I'd do it all over again if I had to." He smiled at me tenderly. "Only maybe slightly differently."

"Only maybe?"

"Well, definitely differently. Maybe no laced wine and no kidnapping." He grinned. "But I'd definitely still like to be tied to you. I'd like to feel the pressure of the rope against my skin as I leaned back into you. Only maybe I'd have us connected the other way. With you on top of me. So that way, when you were wriggling to get loose, you'd be rubbing back and forth on me and . . ."

"Um, I'm still here." Blake put his hand up. "And as delightful as your conversation is, I don't think it's for my ears as well."

"Sorry, Blake." I blushed as I hit Jakob in the shoulder. "He's so inappropriate."

"You love me being inappropriate," Jakob interjected.

"And I wasn't even being inappropriate. Inappropriate would be squeezing your breast or putting my hand in between . . ."

"Jakob!" I screeched. "This whole conversation is inappropriate." I shook my head at him, but my body felt warm. I wanted to pinch myself for being so easy to turn on. Jakob made a face and then gave me a special look.

"We also need to think of what we want to ask Penny."

"Okay, everybody get packing, and let's get to the airport," Jakob said in a no-nonsense voice. As angry as I was at his imperious tone, I was happy that someone else was finally in charge of the investigation.

∽

Jakob and I stood in the family bathroom, just staring at each other. I could hear the different flight announcements through the speakers, and I wondered where Penny was. I wondered what she would do when she saw us. Would she try to run? Or call security and have us arrested?

"Take a deep breath, Bianca, and talk out your worries," Jakob said as he rubbed my shoulder. I looked up in surprise and watched as a wide smile crossed his face. "You didn't think I would forget, did you?" He smiled at me tenderly.

"But I told you that so long ago. We'd barely met. I didn't think you were paying attention to my ramblings about my dad."

"I remember everything you've ever said." He stroked the side of my face. "When will you understand how special you are to me?"

"But I wasn't special to you then."

"You've always been special to me."

"When you first met me?"

"Bianca, I knew you were special the first time I saw you." His voice lowered. "I knew you were special when you played your game with David, and I knew you were more than a pretty face when you spoke to me at that coffee shop that day. I was out of my mind for sitting at the table with you, but I just wanted to be near you. Not just across the room. I wanted to be with you. I wanted you to engage with me."

"I made a fool of myself," I groaned as I remembered that first meeting.

"I thought you were cute."

"I was a bumbling fool." I shook my head. "But you were so handsome. I remember seeing your face under your cap, and I remember my heart racing as I gazed into your gorgeous blue eyes," I said, and blushed as I remembered wanting to make some sort of impression on Jakob that day.

"I guess no matter what happens, we've both still won." Jakob's tone became more serious.

"What do you mean?"

"I mean no matter what we may or may not find out, we still have each other."

"You think we're going to find out something bad?"

"I'm smart enough to know that this whole mystery goes a lot deeper than we think it does. We both got involved because we wanted to honor our mothers and find out what happened to them, but the deeper we go, the more I'm beginning to realize that this isn't about them." Jakob pulled me toward him, and he stared at my face for a few seconds before continuing. "I think that whatever happened to them was because they were a part of this group with our dads. Whatever those men had going was the real problem here."

"I'm scared to hear what Penny has to say." I took a deep breath. "What if something really horrible went down?"

"If my father is really still alive, then I'm sure he didn't disappear for fun." Jakob closed his eyes. "We just have to be prepared for whatever happens. We have to stick together."

"I love you, Jakob. I'm not going anywhere." I grabbed his hand and brought it to my heart. "You're in here, Jakob. You're in my heart, and nothing is going to change that."

"I might be in here as well." Jakob moved his hand to my stomach and rubbed.

"Jakob." I blushed and shook my head. "I'm not pregnant."

"You can't know that for sure." He laughed and was about to say something else when my phone buzzed with an incoming text.

"It's Blake. Penny's here."

"You ready?"

"I'm ready." I nodded and took a deep breath.

"All right, let's go, boss." He nodded at me, and we walked out of the bathroom. A man was standing outside the door, and he gave us a knowing look as we walked out. I wanted to tell him that no, we hadn't been having sex, but

I knew that would have made us look even more guilty. So I settled for glaring at him as we passed.

Heading toward gate 50, I scanned the clusters of seats, looking for Penny or Blake. Finally I saw him at the end of a row, his laptop on his lap. Two seats away sat Mrs. Renee.

"It's her," I muttered to Jakob as we walked. "Shit, Mrs. Renee really is Penny Case!"

"Remember what we agreed in the car," Jakob said lightly. "You'll approach her by yourself. She'll be less intimidated."

"I know." I took a deep breath. "I've got this."

"Don't let her panic, and don't let her get paranoid," he reminded me. "She was so nervous when you met her by yourself, and she was even more anxious when we went back together. Whatever she knows is scaring her, so much that she's leaving the country."

"I don't know that I can calm her fears though. Maybe I'm not the right person for the job."

"I know you are. You know what we need to find out, Bianca. You've got this." Jakob stopped by the bookstore as we'd planned earlier while I continued walking toward Blake and Mrs. Renee. I casually sauntered down the row of chairs, leafing through the *Cosmopolitan* magazine I'd purchased earlier. There was an article about the top ten sex moves for women who wanted to take charge, and I dog-eared the page for later. Hey, I bought the magazine, might as well get my money's worth.

"Mrs. Renee?" I said in feigned surprise as I stopped in front of the older lady, her white hair looking frizzy and wild.

"Bianca?" She looked up at me with wide, displeased eyes. "What are you doing here?" She looked around to see if I was with anyone and frowned up at me. She started fidgeting with her bag, and her movements were making me nervous.

"I'm on my way to Paris. I wanted to get away for a week, see the Eiffel Tower, eat some chocolate croissants . . ." My voice trailed off awkwardly.

"You have money for that?" she asked suspiciously as I sat down next to her. I could feel Blake staring at us as he typed away on his laptop.

"Funnily enough, yes," I said, clearing my throat. "So what has you going to Paris? I'm surprised you're not staying in New York for Larry's trial."

"I, uh, I'm . . ." She looked down at her lap as she mumbled, and I leaned toward her.

"Can I talk frankly with you, Mrs. Renee?" I asked softly. "One woman to another?"

"What do you want?" She looked up at me, a nerve in her face making her right eye twitch.

"I need your help," I said softly and urgently. "I need you to tell me everything you know."

"Know about what?" Her face went white, and I saw her checking her watch. I looked at the time on the departures board, and my heart started pounding. I only had thirty-five minutes until boarding. I needed to get the information I needed from her before that.

"I know you're not married to Larry," I said quickly. "I know your name is Penny Case. I know you're Oliver

Case's little sister. I know you're Steve's aunt. Please stop."
I grabbed her arm as she made to jump up. "I don't want
to hurt you or put you in harm's way. I just need your help.
I need you to tell me what you know. I need to figure out
what's going on here."

"I can't." She shook her head. "There are people watching and recording. Always."

"Not here." I shook my head. "No one is watching and
recording you here."

"They are always recording." Her eyes were wide.

"Please, Penny. They've got Steve involved in this. If you
don't want to help me, won't you help Steve?"

"I didn't know in the beginning." Her voice caught. "I
didn't know how evil they were. They're monsters."

"The people watching you and Larry?" I questioned, remembering she had talked about monsters before.

"No." She grabbed my hand. "Larry and his friends are
the monsters."

"You have to tell me everything you know. I don't want to
be caught up in all of this."

"Oliver was a good boy." She sighed. "Different, but
good and smart. He was so smart. My mother loved him. She
thought he was a baby Einstein, but Father, my father hated
him. He didn't understand him. It was different in those days.
No one was into those sort of things."

"What sort of things?" I frowned. "Being smart?"

"He was my best friend, you know." She looked at me
with a sad face as she ignored my question. "I never had many

friends when I was growing up, but Oliver was always there for me. He always listened. He took care of me after he graduated. I wanted to be an actress. I thought I had talent. Of course I didn't though. Every girl my age wanted to be the next Marilyn Monroe. I thought I had a chance. Oliver supported me. Sent me money every month." She rubbed her forehead. "I thought he was happy. Thought everything was going right for him. He hadn't had the best college experience. He'd fallen in love, but been rejected."

"I didn't know that," I said softly, wanting to say enough so that she would know I was listening, but not too much to stop her from talking.

"I don't think many people did." She continued as if talking to herself. "His first friend was your father. He thought your dad was a stand-up guy until he stole Angelina away from Jeremiah."

"Sorry, what?" I frowned. "Did you say my dad stole my mom away from Jeremiah Bradley? As in, my mother used to date Jeremiah before she dated my dad?"

"Yes." She looked surprised. "You didn't know?"

"No." I shook my head. "I had no idea."

"That's why they set your dad up." Penny rubbed her forehead and sighed. "I didn't think it was a good idea, but who was I to say anything?"

"What do you mean they set my dad up?"

"The inventions." Penny said matter-of-factly. "That's why they were all in your dad's name."

"Why?" My breath caught.

"They wanted your father to be imprisoned for theft. Oliver had all the original patents and paperwork. Jeremiah wanted to teach your father a lesson about stealing from him."

"My father never went to jail though." I frowned. "I don't understand what you're saying."

"Bianca, are you okay?" I heard Jakob's voice next to me, and I wanted to scream as I gazed at Penny's once again stoic face.

"I'm fine." I glared at him. "What are you doing here?"

"Who else is here?" Penny's eyes darted around the gate area.

"Just me." Jakob answered before I could mention Blake.

"Why are you here?" Penny said, frantic now. "I didn't tell her anything. I promise."

"It's fine, Penny," I said softly. "He's with me. He's on our side."

"The Bradleys look out for the Bradleys." She looked into my eyes with a panicked expression.

"I'm not here as a representative of the Bradleys, Penny. I'm here for Bianca." Jakob sat next to me and grabbed my hand. "I know I shouldn't have come, but I didn't want to leave you here sitting alone. Not after what happened yesterday."

"What happened?" Penny asked frantically.

I explained quickly. "Steve and Rosie tried to take me to go and meet someone, but they didn't tell me why."

"Steve's a good boy," Penny said with a frown. "I failed him." She pursed her lips and mumbled something to herself.

"What did you just say?" I asked her softly.

"I said that I regret the day I ever introduced him to Roma."

"She's Larry's daughter, isn't she?"

"Yes. A monster from a monster." She sighed. "I didn't see the signs. I didn't believe until it was too late."

"Until what was too late? What happened?"

"Like I was saying, it all started when your mom left Jeremiah for your dad," Penny said with a hint of blame in her voice.

"Your mom dated my dad?" Jakob looked at me in shock. "Before she dated your dad?"

"She was just explaining that when you interrupted us." I put my hand on his thigh and squeezed it, hard. The last thing I needed was for him to freak Penny out and make her clam up. Not when she was so close to telling me everything she knew.

"Yes. It was quite the scandal." Penny nodded. "Apparently, Jeremiah was extremely upset by the betrayal."

"So my dad loved Angelina Walker?" Jakob said thoughtfully.

"Oh, no." Penny laughed bitterly. "Jeremiah Bradley didn't do love. In fact, he didn't even particularly like Angelina, but he knew that Nick did. From the first time he laid eyes on her, Nick was in love. That's why Jakob started dating her. He wanted to be in a position of power over Nick. He wanted to show Nick that he was number one."

"What?" I gasped. "That's awful."

"That was Jeremiah. On the surface, he was the nicest, most welcoming person, but he always had another motivation. He was born with a hidden agenda."

"How do you know all of this?" Jakob asked with a frown. "Did you grow up with them?"

"I'm sure Oliver told her," I said quickly, but Penny shook her head.

"Actually, no, it all came from Larry," she said with a twisted smile. "That's always been his problem. He's got a big mouth. He lets certain things slip that he shouldn't. Oh, he hid the big things, but I'm not dumb. I could figure them out."

"Larry told you?" I prodded, hoping she would go further in her conversation.

"They called them Beauty and Charm," she said.

"Who?" Jakob's voice was tense.

"Larry and Jeremiah."

"No, who did they call Beauty and Charm?" Jakob questioned, and my heart almost stopped as I realized that that wasn't the first time I'd heard that term.

"Angelina and Nick," she said impatiently. "Angelina was beauty, and Nick was charm. The perfect couple." She shook her head. "But nothing's perfect, is it?"

"That's what one of the notes said," I interrupted, and looked at Jakob. "'Beauty and Charm. One survives. One is destroyed. What are your odds?'" I blinked up at him. "That can't be a coincidence, can it?"

"I don't believe in coincidence." His eyes looked into

mine intently. "Whoever sent you that note chose those words on purpose."

"Yes, it has to have a deeper meaning."

"Who could have sent it?" Jakob said, and I shook my head.

"Maybe Larry? Or Jeremiah?" My voice sounded weak even to my own ears.

"Jeremiah twisted up everything. And everyone," Penny interjected. "I wish I'd never let him mentor Steve."

"Why did you get with Larry?" I asked her softly, not understanding how she could still be protecting the man she called a monster.

"I didn't realize he was bad when I met him. He was saving me. Oliver had died, and Larry appeared out of nowhere. He told me he was one of Oliver's best friends and that Oliver had been murdered by powerful men. He told me they would come after me next, but if I left with him, he could protect me. I believed him." She shrugged. "I didn't have any way to support myself after Oliver passed away. I never made it as an actress."

"But what about Steve? Who looked after him?"

"Steve was with a foster family." She looked away from me, and I could see shame filling her eyes.

"Even before Oliver died?"

"My brother wasn't a good father. And I was too selfish to take him on. I regret that now. Maybe he wouldn't have so many issues."

"Issues?"

"He's crazy," she said with a straight face. "I tried to help."

"How did you try to help?" Jakob asked softly.

"I sent a letter to Jeremiah Bradley. I told him what I knew. I knew some things, you know. Some things that could ruin him. I wanted a million dollars. I was going to give it to Steve."

The letter! "What happened?"

"He told me he was going to look after Steve. He told me that he'd treat Steve like his own son. He told me he'd love Steve like his own. I thought that would be good. That's what Oliver would have wanted. It would have made his heart soar."

"So what happened?"

"Jeremiah didn't care about Steve. He just wanted to shut me up. And he did. I didn't realize the truth until it was too late." She buried her face in her hands. "It was too late for all of us." She looked up and pursed her lips. "That's why I'm going to France. I want a new life. I wanted Steve to come with me, but he said he can't go."

"He knows you're his aunt?"

"He knows a lot of things." She shrugged.

The loudspeaker crackled to life: *Bonsoir, ladies and gentlemen. We now welcome our first-class passengers to board Air France flight 250 to Paris.* . . .

"Penny, has Larry ever mentioned to you that Jeremiah might still be alive?" I asked her urgently. We were running out of time.

"Jeremiah still alive?" Her eyes stilled, and she sat upright and clutched her bag to her side. "Why would you say that?"

"Because of the person Steve wants me to meet," I said again, willing her to be completely honest.

"I don't know." She shook her head. "I will tell you one thing though. Right before your father passed on, he came to visit me. Nick wanted to know what I knew about the fact that all the patents were in his name, even though Oliver had been the chief designer behind the self-painter."

"So he knew he'd been set up?" I said with a frown.

"Your dad was a smart man. He was the one who made me realize Larry didn't have my best interests at heart." She leaned forward. "He said to me, be careful of those who seek to help you. They may do more harm than good. Nick was—"

"Can you say that again?" I interrupted her.

"He said, be careful of those who seek to help you. They may do more harm than good," she repeated, a little miffed that I'd cut her off.

"That's what I thought." I turned to Jakob. "That's what the man said to me, the one who called me on my dad's phone! That day the fake policeman came to my apartment after Dad died."

"Are you sure he used the same words?" Jakob's eyes were burning with intensity.

"I'm positive. This is huge. Beauty and charm and now this." I shook my head. "Who was behind the messages?"

"I assumed David and Rosie, but now I don't know." Jakob shook his head. "I really don't."

"You both have to be careful," Penny said, and I was about to answer her when I saw Blake jump up and approach us.

"I'm sorry." He apologized as he stopped in front of us. "But I couldn't not come over, not with so little time left."

"Who is this?" Penny looked frightened as she gazed at Blake.

"He's a friend. What's going on, Blake?" I frowned. Penny was even more uncomfortable now, shifting in her seat as if she were about to get up and run away.

"Remember the letter your dad left you?" Blake said to me.

"Yeah, why?"

"It said, *As I've gone through my papers and recalled various conversations from the days before her death, it has occurred to me that there may have been people that wanted to see me incapacitated. People that knew that your mother's death would change everything in my life. My darling, I may not be able to leave you riches in the bank, but go through the papers in the box and you might find the truth*," Blake said quickly, and my jaw dropped as he repeated from memory a part of my dad's letter. "What can I say? I have a photographic memory." He laughed, but then his expression changed. "It was a clue, Bianca! I think that the papers he left you, the patents and all that stuff, weren't for you to get a share of the company, but more to right the wrongs of the past. Your dad said *incapacitated*. We thought he meant dead. What if he meant imprisoned? He told you to find the truth in the box. We know now that the truth is that he didn't create the self-painter. We also know that Jeremiah was conniving to get him imprisoned." He looked at Penny and smiled weakly. "Sorry, I was eavesdropping."

Penny's face was blank as she stared back at Blake. I was pretty sure she was still in shock and wondering who else was going to pop up as part of the group.

"That makes a lot of sense." Jakob looked at Blake with respect.

"So then, what you're saying is that my father *wanted* me to talk to Penny?" I asked, trying to follow along. I was becoming extremely overwhelmed.

"I'm saying that we've been looking at the clues all wrong. We assumed that every clue was about you and Jakob. What if the clues all relate to the past? What if all the clues are about your father and mother? We know that the beauty and charm clue is about them. One is destroyed and one survives, right?"

"Yeah." I nodded.

"So, who was destroyed and who survived?"

"Well, Bianca's mom died in the car crash, right?" Jakob said. "So presumably, Angelina was destroyed, and her dad, Nick, survived."

"And maybe it points to the fact that Angelina was murdered," Blake said. "To destroy means to put an end to something."

"So then my mother's car crash really wasn't an accident . . . which is what we thought," I chimed in.

"Her car crash wasn't an accident," Penny said, and stood up. "I have to go."

"You can't!" I jumped up. "I know you have more to tell us."

"I have to go." She shook her head. "I'm sorry, Bianca."

"Please!"

"I've helped you as much as I can." She grabbed my hands. "That's why I told you about Roma, the last time you saw me. You think I did that by accident? You think I didn't know what I was doing?"

"You knew that Roma was Rosie?"

"I told you that Maxwell screwed us all, remember? I told you they were all thick as thieves. I *told* you."

"You knew." I nodded. "You knew Larry was Maxwell. You were telling me that he wasn't to be trusted as well?"

"I knew the papers he left you weren't to help you. They were going to harm you. I didn't want to give them to you. I didn't want you to fall for his trap. I told you that you shouldn't be there. I told you." Her grasp tightened; she was nearly crushing my fingers, but I was afraid to do anything to discourage her confession.

"You did." I nodded.

"Your father wouldn't want you to own a third of Bradley Inc." Her voice was low. "He hated the company. He said he was manipulated, just like Oliver was. Just like Macy. Just like Joanie. Just like all of them."

"What about Larry?" I asked softly.

"No one manipulates Larry." She shook her head, her eyes boring into mine as if trying to implant knowledge right into my brain. "I have to go." She leaned over and gave me a quick hug. "I'm sorry, Bianca. Good luck." As she pulled away, she whispered in my ear. "There's a reason Larry's the last one standing."

Then she dashed for the gate and disappeared down the jetway, leaving me to wonder: Where did we go from here?

nine

Nicholas London
Decades Ago

"We need to talk about this, Nick." Jeremiah's voice was calm, but I could tell from the look in his eyes that he was angry.

"I have nothing to say, Jeremiah. I don't want your shares. I don't want your money."

"You can't live forever, Nick. You can't provide for Bianca forever. You need money. Don't you want to protect her?"

"Protect her?" I said, my heart stopping. "That's an odd choice of words." I moved closer to him and looked him in the eyes. I no longer recognized my friend. This man was consumed by greed, by lies, and by vengeance. I saw that now.

"Everyone has a price, Nick. Every action has a consequence." Jeremiah shrugged and stood up. "I'm just trying to help you so you don't make any mistakes. You need to think of your family. You're all Bianca has left now."

"Yes, I am." I stood up as well, and we faced each other as two enemies. Our friendship was now officially over. I was David to his Goliath, and I knew that I couldn't back down.

"Think about your actions carefully, Nick. There will come a day when you'll die and Bianca will be all alone. Left to fend for herself." He tilted his head. "And we all know what happens when little piggies are around wolves."

I turned around then and walked to the door of his office. I looked at Larry sitting in the corner, a smug look on his face, and it was then I knew—there was only one way to fix this. If it didn't work, both Bianca and I would be imprisoned. Or dead. And I wasn't going to let that happen.

part 2

ten

Bianca London
Present Day

Anticipation can kill you, or drive you crazy. I was pretty confident that I was driving both Blake and Jakob crazy with my constant muttering. While our talk with Penny had been enlightening, it hadn't helped us as much as we'd hoped it would.

"Are you ready for tonight?" Jakob kissed the side of my neck as he rubbed my upper thigh in the back of the limousine that was taking us to the ball.

"No." I shifted on the black leather seat and turned to him. "Do you think we're making a mistake?" I pulled out my cell phone from my purse and reread the text message that Rosie had sent that morning. *I hope you got the invitation. We expect to see you and Jakob tonight.*

"Stop worrying, Bianca." The tip of Jakob's tongue was in my ear, and I squirmed away from him.

"What are you doing?" I looked at him in frustration. "This is possibly the most important night of our lives. Of course I'm worried and nervous, and I don't understand how you can be sucking on my neck right now. Is that really all that's on your mind?"

"Bianca, this is not the most important night of our lives. Thus far, the most important moment of our lives has been the day we met, and the most important *night* of our lives will be the night we're married."

"You're such a romantic." I shook my head. "At least you didn't say the most important night of our lives was the first night we had sex."

"That's up there as well." He grinned at me, and I felt his hand sliding up my leg. I caught it as he tried to insert his fingers between my thighs.

"No, I don't think so, Jakob." I couldn't stop myself from giggling. "I'm not about to have sex with you in the back of this limo."

"Hmm, that's a good idea. That wasn't even what I was thinking." He licked his lips. "I was just hoping to calm your nerves."

"With your fingers in between my thighs?" I tilted my head up at him.

"Not exactly." He leaned down and whispered in my ear. "The goal was to have my fingers inside of you, pleasuring you until you came. I find that having an intense orgasm always makes you calmer."

"Jakob!" My jaw dropped as I squirmed. "You're unbelievable." I was about to say something else when the limo stopped. "We're here?" I said in surprise as I looked out the window.

"Don't you feel better?" He grinned at me, and we waited for the chauffeur to open the door.

"You did that just to distract me?" I asked with a soft smile, my heart melting as I gazed at him. "You weren't really planning to finger me in the car?"

"Whatever you want to think." He grinned at me and then turned away as the door opened. I watched as Jakob slid from the car and held a hand out to me as I followed, my heart racing fast and my panties slightly wet.

"You have your mask ready?" he asked me as we stood there and the limo pulled off.

"Yes," I said, and placed it over my head. The elastic band rubbed against the back of my ears uncomfortably, and I watched as he slid his peacock-blue mask over his face. The blue matched the hue of his eyes, and his eyes seemed to sparkle as he stared at me. "You're excited, aren't you?"

"I'd be lying if I said I wasn't." He nodded.

"How can you be excited, Jakob?" I shook my head. "We have no idea what's going to happen tonight. Rosie and Steve are almost certainly setting us up. We have no idea who they want us to meet, if they even *have* anyone for us to meet." I froze as I looked up at him. "What if they don't? What if they want to kidnap us?"

"That's not going to happen." Jakob's eyes narrowed. "First, I'm stronger than I look."

"But you look strong," I said, confused.

"Exactly." He smiled. "And I'm even stronger than that."

"Oh, you're silly." I shook my head as I giggled. "I don't know why I'm laughing. There's nothing funny about this situation."

"Let the nervous energy go, Bianca. Plus you'll have your BFF Blake here, and I'm sure he can save you if I can't."

"Blake is smart, but I don't think he's exactly Mr. Universe."

"Oh, not much muscles?" he said casually.

"None at all." I laughed.

"How do you know?" He frowned. "Have you seen him naked?" His tone was surly, and I smiled inwardly. I knew it was mean of me, but I loved seeing a jealous Jakob, even if he irritated me at times. Did he really think Blake was a threat?

"Only once or twice," I said innocently, and held back a laugh as Jakob's lips turned down.

"When did you see him naked?" he demanded, and I smiled at him gently.

"When we had our one-night stand." I adjusted my clutch in my hands and then continued. "Oops, I guess two-night stand. Is that even possible? Can one have a two-night stand?"

"What?" His voice was loud, and I couldn't stop myself from laughing heartily. My laughter only increased as Jakob did a slow burn.

"I'm joking, goofy." I touched his jacket lapel lightly, and I could feel his heart racing. "I haven't slept with Blake, and I've never seen him naked. Stop acting like a jealous boyfriend."

"So you haven't slept with him?"

"You know that!" I exclaimed. "I told you that when you first met him. You know he's just my friend."

"Hmm," Jakob responded.

"What is your problem, Jakob?" I sighed, no longer laughing. "We don't have time for this right now."

"No problem." He sighed and grabbed my arm. "Let's go in now. It's time to get this party started."

"My stomach is rumbling," I said lightly. "I'm so nervous."

"I know a way to stop the nerves."

"Oh?" I looked over at him, wondering if he had some sort of pill to give me. "What's that?"

"Sex."

"Jakob!" I hissed at him. "Not that again. I'm not about to fuck you at a masquerade ball. Especially not tonight."

"What if I told you that I've been dreaming for over a year about pushing you up against a wall, sliding that dress up and entering you swiftly?"

"Huh?" I said, confused.

"I know you attended the last Bradley Ball." He leaned toward me. "And I wanted you badly then as well. In fact, I even had a dream after that night that you and I were—"

"Okay, I get it." I blushed and cut him off as another couple passed us. "You never told me that before."

"I didn't think it was important until now."

"And it's important now, why?" I gave him a side glance.

"Because tonight it might happen."

"Jakob!"

"What?" He laughed. "I'm still a man, and you're my woman."

"Tonight is not the time to be thinking about kinky sex."

"I disagree."

"You think tonight *is* the night to be thinking about kinky sex?"

"No, that's not what I disagree with. I disagree with your characterization of kinky sex. Sex at a ball isn't what I classify as kinky." He paused. "That is unless you want to tie me to something again."

"Jakob!"

"What? Did you bring some handcuffs?" he whispered, and laughed.

"Focus, Jakob. We're nearly inside."

"Whatever you do, don't let them separate us. And keep your cell phone on." Jakob frowned as he glanced at the high slit in my dress. "You look sexy as hell, by the way." He growled. "Way too sexy."

"Shouldn't that be a good thing?" I asked with a smile as I reapplied my deep red lipstick.

"Not in this case. Not when you know how horny I am." He shook his head and grabbed my hand, and we made our way into the main ballroom, where the ball was being held.

The room was dark and packed when we arrived. I watched some of the couples on the dance floor gliding across the room like swans, sensuous and graceful. The mood seemed light and cheery, and I could hear people laughing while exchanging flirtatious smiles and surreptitious fondlings. A few couples kissed passionately in the corners of the room, and I stared, mesmerized, at one man who was publicly groping his date's breasts.

"How are you feeling?" Jakob asked me lightly as he took my hand.

"Overwhelmed," I said honestly. "I feel like we're in an action movie like *True Lies*. I'm Jamie Lee Curtis, and you're Arnold Schwarzenegger."

"I'll be back," Jakob said in a deep Austrian accent, and I laughed.

"Be serious, Jakob," I said, and chastised him. Now was not the time for us to be goofing off. "Can you see Blake?" I asked him softly as we both looked around.

"I don't know," he said. "Can you text him and see if he's here? I don't know who anyone is right now. It's so dark in here, and the masks aren't helping."

"I don't understand masquerade balls," I said as I tried to make out Rosie and David. "What's exciting about wearing a disguise?"

"You tell me." He shrugged. "You're the history buff."

"I don't know about masked balls." I shook my head as we walked around the perimeter of the room.

"I think masked balls were started by men who liked

kinky sex and didn't want anyone to know," Jakob said as
he pulled me toward him. "It's the only thing that makes
sense."

"There's a man staring at us," I said softly into his ear as I
felt someone staring me down. "Across the room to the right
of us. He's wearing a bright red mask." I shivered as I looked
at him. "He reminds me of the devil."

"So maybe my father is alive after all," Jakob joked, but
neither one of us laughed. He looked toward the right, but
the man had already disappeared.

"It might have been Steve or David," I said softly, but I
wasn't convinced. The man's stare had been intent, and his
body stocky. Much stockier than Steve's and David's. "Do
you think we were stupid to come here?" I said, suddenly
feeling really afraid. What had I been thinking? I felt like a
sheep in the lion's den.

"What other option did we have?" Jakob said, his voice
serious for the first time that evening. "Right now, Steve and
Rosie are holding all the cards. But we know some of those
cards, and we have a contingency plan if they try to cheat."

"What contingency plan?"

"We have Blake."

"What's Blake going to do?" I mumbled as I looked
around the room. Blake had no strength. If this was a setup,
we were dead.

"Bianca, listen to me. We're going to be okay. I promise.
I'm not going to let anything happen to you." His eyes bored
into mine. "I have five men in here with us."

"What?" I looked at him in shock. "What five men?"

"Don't worry about it, but I've got us covered."

"Why didn't you tell me?"

"Sometimes the less you know, the easier it is."

"You can't keep things from me!"

"Important things," Jakob said casually as he looked around. "I won't keep important things from you, but this wasn't something you needed to know. The fewer people who know, the better for us."

"Fine," I said as we made our way around the room. "What should we do?"

"We need to dance." He grabbed my hand. "And wait. I'm sure Rosie and Steve will make themselves known to us."

"And then we meet your dad or whoever."

"Yeah." He nodded. "If he's behind all of this, I just don't know what I'll do."

I just nodded and allowed Jakob to guide me to the dance floor. After a few minutes of us moving silently to the music, I asked him, "What are you thinking?"

"I'm thinking that dancing with you here is even more magical than I thought it would be," he whispered in my ear as he tightened his grip on my waist. His thighs pressed against mine as we glided across the room, and I held on to his shoulder, trying to concentrate on my steps. Jakob was a smooth dancer, and I could see that the movements came effortlessly to him. I needed to work a little harder, as I didn't have natural rhythm.

"I didn't know you were such a romantic," I said

eventually, willing myself to relax, but my eyes were on high alert as we danced. I hadn't seen the man with the red mask again, and I wasn't sure who anyone else was, as everyone was in costume.

"I never used to be," he said as his right hand moved up and down my back. "I suspect that you're the one who brought it out in me."

"Like Jeremiah brought it out in your mom?" I said softly.

"I guess so." He nodded, his voice sad. "I just don't get it. By all accounts, Jeremiah was a horrible man. I mean, what did my mother see in him? Why would she love a man like that?"

"It's like you said before, the heart doesn't choose who to fall in love with."

"But still, some of the things my mom has told me don't add up." He stopped suddenly, and I stumbled to the side. I gasped as I was about to hit the ground, but he scooped me up in time.

"Sorry," he said as he held me to him. "I just remembered something."

"I hope it was something good." I pouted at him. "I nearly fell."

"It's a poem my mom wrote."

"And?" I looked up at him. "I love your mom's poems, but was it important enough to stop in the middle of the dance floor?"

"Come with me." He grabbed my hand and pulled me

to the corner of the room, away from any of the groups that were starting to assemble.

"What's going on?" I frowned.

"So this poem—I never thought about it before. It didn't touch me like some of the others. But I think it might be the most helpful."

"Okay? How? Please enlighten me," I said, frustrated. "What are you talking about, Jakob?"

"Listen to this," he said, and he closed his eyes. I stood there waiting for him to continue, but he was silent.

"Um, what am I listening to?" I asked, annoyed. "The sound of silence? Is that the clue? Was your mom into Simon and Garfunkel?"

"Bianca." Jakob laughed. "I'm trying to remember the lines."

"Oh, sorry."

"The poem has nothing to do with Simon and Garfunkel."

"I'm listening," I said. "And hopefully, not to the sounds of silence," I joked. Jakob just smiled and cleared his throat.

"'This man, this man of mine, is not mine. This man, this man of mine, is generous and kind. This man, this man I love, is all I could ever ask for. This man, this charming man, is wise and thoughtful. This man, this best friend of mine, is never going to be mine. This man, this man, this man, this charming man. This man of mine. This man that is not mine. This man was never mine. This is the man that I love.'"

"Wow, sad," I said as I felt tears welling up in my eyes, and my heart grew heavy. How sad it must have been for Jakob's mother to have been in love with someone that didn't love her.

"Did anything stick out to you?" Jakob asked me, and I thought for a moment.

"Um, that the man wasn't hers?"

"Aside from that, Bianca. Think."

"I don't know," I snapped. "What stuck out to you?"

"The word *charming*. It appears twice," he said, his tone excited. "It's as if *charming* was synonymous with the man she was talking about. The man she was in love with. Remember what the note from the island said?"

"Beauty and Charm. One survives and one is destroyed." My face paled. I could feel every beat of my heart pounding through my chest as we stood there. "So what are you saying?"

"Just think about it for a few seconds. My mom was in love with a charming man. And the note says that he was with a beauty." He touched my face and rubbed my cheek gently as his eyes surveyed me. "And I can confirm that if you look anything like your mother, she must have been really beautiful."

"So you think your mom was having an affair with my dad?"

"Yes, no, well, I don't know exactly. I think it's a possibility."

He reached down and gripped my hands. "What I do think is that my mom wasn't talking about Jeremiah. He isn't known by anyone to be charming. The only person at this point who makes sense is your dad. I think that she was in love with him. And that had to be for a reason." His eyes gazed into mine searchingly, and I knew he was wondering how I felt inside. He was most probably wondering if I was going to have some sort of nervous breakdown. "I just think that maybe both of our parents had secrets we knew nothing about."

"And you think this confirms that my mom was having an affair with Jeremiah by default or something?"

"No." He shook his head. "I don't really know all the facts, but I think it confirms a lot more than anything to do with affairs."

"Oh?"

"It means that your dad was the man she always loved. Your dad was the one that got away. He was the one, not Jeremiah. It makes sense, if you think about it. The poems describe a man who's kind, sweet, charming, her friend. That didn't make sense in relation to Jeremiah, but it would make sense for *your* father."

"Your mom loved my dad?" I frowned. "My dad was the one who broke her heart?" I said guiltily, and looked up at Jakob with a worried expression. Was he going to hate me again? This wasn't the island, where we'd been strangers—if he blamed me now, my heart would break.

"I think so." He nodded. "He's the one she wishes she could have been with. When I was younger, she told me that outside forces kept her from being with the man that she loved. She blamed it on him wanting to marry someone better than her. I always assumed she meant someone richer because I assumed she was talking about Macy Vanderbilt, but what if she just meant your mom? That would explain her vehemence toward your family. Why she always seemed to hate your mom so much."

"She was jealous," I said, and sighed. "I'm sorry, I had no idea."

"It's not your fault." He shook his head, his tone light. "And it's not your dad's fault either. From all accounts, your mom and dad loved each other more than anything in the world. Maybe they were friends. Maybe my mom wanted what they had. My mom told me when she was older that she regretted some of the decisions she'd made."

"I wonder which ones?"

"I wish I knew." He sighed. "Sometimes I think that our parents didn't know the sky from the ground."

"Yeah. . . ." My voice trailed off. I didn't know what to say.

"It's a good thing we're different," he said, grabbing my hand, his finger rubbing the inside of my wrist.

"We are?"

"Yeah, we are." He nodded. "We're different because I can tell you with all certainty that there is nothing that can stop my love for you and that there is nothing I wouldn't do to be with you."

"You're just saying that," I said, but my heart was racing at his words.

"You're my favorite person, Bianca." He clasped my fingers with his. "You're my favorite person in the world. The only person that has ever made me smile for no reason at all. The only person that has filled my heart with such love that sometimes I don't even recognize who I am anymore."

"You're going to make me cry." I bit down on my lower lip. "And this is not the place for me to cry."

"No one will see you if you cry," he said, his voice wavering with emotion. "You're so strong, Bianca."

"I'm not strong."

"You are. I didn't see you cry once on the island." His voice held awe, and I could feel him staring at me. "You're so much stronger than you think you are."

"I suppose I have to be. I don't feel strong though," I said as my eyes got heavy and my throat felt raw. "I don't feel strong at all. I feel sad and tired and stressed, and I don't ever know if anything I'm doing is going to be good enough. Will I ever find the answers to my mother's death? Will I ever find out if all of this was in vain? I just want to know why my mother died! But I feel like I'm no closer to the truth than when I started weeks ago. Yes, I'm finding out things that are shocking and maybe helpful in some way, but where's the end? What if we never get answers?"

"We'll get them." He wrapped his arms around my waist and pulled me toward him. "If I have to spend my entire fortune getting you the answers you're looking for, I will."

"How did I get so lucky?" I leaned forward and kissed him.

"No one got luckier than me." He kissed me back, and I felt his hands slide down to caress my ass.

"Jakob," I whimpered against his mouth as he pushed me back against the wall and pressed his full length against me.

"Yes, Bianca?" He drew my hands up and flattened them against the wall behind me. I could feel my heart racing as he pushed himself into me harder and kissed my neck.

"Do you want to get lucky?" I whispered teasingly. All I could focus on was the fact that I was with the sexiest man in the world and that he was all mine.

"Are you joking?" he groaned as his left hand entered the slit of my dress and he ran his fingers up my thigh. I changed my stance slightly to give him easier access, groaning as he slid his hand all the way up to my thong and lightly rubbed between my legs. My body pulsed in reaction to his fingers, and Jakob's heartbeat throbbed next to mine.

"Would I joke about that?" I murmured as I curled my hand around his neck and pulled his face closer to kiss him. His lips clung to mine longingly, and I ran my fingers through his silky hair as he continued getting me wet and excited with his fingers. And then he pushed his tongue into my mouth at the exact moment that he slipped a finger inside of me, and I felt myself drowning in the moment. Everything was turning me on: the roughness of his fingers inside of my smooth wetness, the feel of his hard cock against my stomach, the plunging of his guided, yet silky tongue as he assaulted the senses of my mouth, the woodsy masculine scent of his cologne, the soft tresses of his luxurious hair against my fingers, the rapid beating of his heart next to mine.

"Fuck me, Jakob," I muttered as I pulled away from his kiss and looked directly into his eyes. "Take me now."

Jakob didn't wait to comply. I reached down and rubbed the front of his pants, quickly undoing his zipper. He was already hard as I slipped my fingers into his pants and I grinned with satisfaction that I'd been able to turn him on so quickly. I looked around the room to see if anyone had noticed what we were up to in our darkened corner, but I couldn't see anyone watching us. "I'm a dirty bitch," I whispered to myself as I realized that being in this room full of other disguised people was part of the excitement.

"Turn around," Jakob said before spinning me to face the wall. "Lean forward and tilt your ass up." He pulled my hair as he whispered into my ear and pushed himself up against me. I felt him moving the length of my dress to the side and once again I felt his fingers rubbing me, getting me wet and ready for his manhood. "Oh, Bianca . . . ," he groaned as I felt the tip of his cock rubbing against my wet opening. I felt him glide into me smoothly and determinedly, and his cock pushed in and out of me quickly. All I could think about was how good it felt to have him inside of me. I clutched the wall and closed my eyes. I could almost forget that I was in a ball-room. I could almost pretend that I couldn't hear the sounds of music pulsating from the speakers a couple of meters away from me. All I could really hear was the guttural sound of Jakob breathing as he filled me up. His movements were graceful and rough, and I almost collapsed as he grabbed hold of my hips and slammed into me hard. I wasn't sure how much longer I could take the intense pleasure before bursting into orgasm, and that made me almost sad. I didn't want it to end. I didn't want this exquisite feeling to leave me, ever. I loved the feel of him inside of me. I loved the feel of his pants rubbing against my ass as he entered me. I loved the pressure of his fingers on my hips. I even loved the cool breeze on my face from the AC vent above me. I loved the fact that we were doing something so taboo in public, and no one knew. I loved the fact that even if someone knew, I didn't care.

"I'm going to come, Bianca." He grunted and increased his movements. I felt him slam into me hard three more times before he exploded inside of me, and that's when I erupted, my body shaking against him and the wall as I orgasmed. I rested my forehead against the wall for a few seconds and then felt him withdrawing from me and pulling my skirt back down before he turned me around and kissed me hard. "I fucking love you, Bianca London."

"For letting you fuck me in a packed room?"

"No, for being you," he said simply, and I raised an eyebrow at him. "*And* for letting me make love to you at a masquerade ball." He laughed. "That was even hotter than I'd imagined it."

eleven

"There you are." Blake hurried over to us a few minutes later, and I blushed, wondering if he could tell what we'd been up to. He looked sharp in his black tuxedo and sparkly gold mask, and I smiled up at him, pretending that I hadn't made love in this very spot just moments ago.

"How did you know it was us?" I said, surprised.

"I'd recognize you anywhere," he said softly, and I shifted uncomfortably as Jakob gave me a knowing look.

"I'm glad you made it." I changed the subject. "I haven't seen Rosie or Steve yet, but some guy in a red mask was staring at us, so I'm sure they know we're here."

"Which means they most probably know I'm here too, now that I've come up to you." Blake made a face. "That blows my cover."

"So why did you come up to us?" I asked him softly.

"I've got more news, and I wasn't thinking."

"This is why I hired the other men," Jakob said matter-of-factly.

"The chances of Blake making it in without talking to us or making eye contact were far too slim, and I'm sure every move we make is being watched." He touched my arm lightly. "You forget that I've been on the other side."

"Oh, I didn't forget," I said, and turned back to Blake. "So what did you find out?"

"The love child. I know who it is. I know who David's secret half sibling is."

"Just David's?" I asked, my mind racing. "I thought it was David and Jakob's half sibling?"

"I was wrong about that." Blake was speaking fast, stumbling over his words. "The blackmail letter said 'We have a child that shares our DNA.' I automatically assumed that meant the child was Jeremiah's, and thus David and Jakob's sibling. However, that wasn't right. The child was only related to David."

"How is that possible?" I said, confused. "If Jeremiah fathered a child, why wouldn't it be Jakob's sibling as well?"

"Because in this case, the child wasn't directly a result of the cheating," Blake said dramatically.

"Then why the blackmail letter?" I frowned. "And who was cheating?"

"You're talking about Macy, right?" Jakob looked at Blake, who nodded.

"Yes, I'm talking about Macy."

"So who's this mysterious child of Macy?" Jakob asked, his face looking intense. I wondered how he was feeling in this moment. If he felt as overwhelmed as I did.

"Steve!" Blake said excitedly. "Macy Vanderbilt is listed on his original birth certificate."

"What are you talking about, original?" Jakob frowned. "How many does he have?" He paused and looked at me glaring at him and grinned.

"His first birth certificate was deleted from the system, and a new one was created," Blake said. "And the mother was listed as unknown."

"And Oliver Case was listed as the dad?" I asked.

"No, there was no dad listed. Ever." Blake shook his head.

I was confused. "So no parents were listed on his birth certificate?"

"That's correct." He nodded. "I have a source at CPS and got access to the files from when Steve was put into foster care as a baby. Someone in children's services never shredded the original birth certificate."

"I don't get it," I said. "So Oliver and Macy had an affair. Macy had the baby and then put it up for adoption?" I said, looking at Jakob to see if he understood it better than I did.

"Why would Penny send my father a blackmail letter if it was Macy who had the affair?" Jakob asked Blake. "And why did Macy have an affair with Oliver and then give the baby up for adoption?"

"Why is a good question," a voice said from behind us, and we all jumped. Steve stood there in all his awkward glory.

He wasn't wearing a tuxedo or a mask, and he looked dreadfully out of place in his blue jeans and black shirt.

"Steve," I said, my tone weak as I could feel the blood racing through my veins. This was it, then. This was the moment I'd been waiting for since I'd last seen Steve and Rosie.

"Fancy seeing you here, Bianca London," he said, and then laughed. His face looked weirdly contorted, and I shivered as I stared at him. "We must stop bumping into each other like this. It almost seems like you're following me around. Everywhere I go, there you are. It's almost like fate."

"Almost," I said lightly. He stopped laughing and sneered.

"I mean it had to have been fate that had us on a deserted island together." He paused. "Oh wait, that wasn't fate. That was your boyfriend paying me to terrorize you."

"What do you want, Steve?" Jakob's voice was harsh. "We're here now. Show us whoever you want to show us, and let's get this over with."

"You'd like that, wouldn't you?" Steve narrowed his eyes. "You're not calling the shots tonight, Bradley."

"And you are?" Jakob sneered back at him. "You're not in charge of anything, Steve. You know that, right? Rosie is playing you."

"I am in charge." Steve's face twisted up angrily, and he made a move toward Jakob. "You have no idea who you're talking to."

"What is it you want, Steve?" I asked him softly. "Maybe we can help you. I know you must have had a hard life."

"A hard life?" He looked at me in distaste. "My mother was a whore who cheated on her husband. My father was a pathetic useless man who tried to play games to get what he wanted, but it backfired on him. They gave me up as a baby, and it was only when I became a teenager that I got a chance. Jeremiah Bradley hired me as his special assistant. Oh, the irony." He moved his face to inches from mine. "You want to know what a hard life is? Being called a love child when you're anything but loved."

"I'm sorry," I said softly. "I'm truly sorry that you're a victim, Steve. We're all victims here. I'm not your enemy."

"I could love someone like you," he said softly, and lightly touched the side of my face. I shook my head slightly as I saw Jakob about to make a move toward us. "I could spend my days in your arms as you kissed me and told me everything was going to be all right." His eyes gazed into mine softly for a few seconds, and then he stepped back. "I see why he loves you so much."

"I do love her," Jakob said softly, and Steve turned to him with a sneer.

"I'm not talking about you." He glanced at Blake. "You must be the best friend." He glanced up and down at Blake and laughed. "And you wonder why you never got the girl. You look like a loser."

"Steve," I said, wondering what was going on. "Who do you want us to meet?" I touched his arm, and he turned to me with a blank expression.

"Who do I want you to meet?" His accent changed to

English, as it had the first time I'd met him, and I wondered if he was truly all right in the head. There was a distinct possibility that Steve was insane. At first, I'd thought it was all an act, but I was starting to realize that this crazy ran bone-deep.

"Steve, you and Rosie wanted to take me to meet someone and then told me to bring Jakob to this ball."

"I can't believe you came." He shook his head. "I can't believe you listened to us."

"Is this a trap?" I leaned forward. "Please tell me, are Rosie and David trying to trap us?"

"David?" He started laughing. "David?" He fell forward as his laughter took over his whole body. "David doesn't know anything. He's a fool."

"He's your brother," Blake spoke up.

"He's no brother of mine." Steve looked at him in disgust. "I should have killed him."

"Why?" Jakob asked. "Why did you want to kill him?"

"Because." Steve shrugged. "Just because."

"What happened with our parents was wrong," Jakob continued. "And you were a victim, Steve, but Rosie doesn't have your best interests at heart. She's using you."

"You think I don't know that?" He took a pill out of his pocket and swallowed it. "That dumb bitch has no idea what I have planned."

"For us or for her?" I said softly.

"Jakob was right, you know. Your parents ruined everything." Steve suddenly turned to me with a menacing look.

"What do you mean?" My heart thudded, and my whole body suddenly felt cold, and my hands were clammy.

"I know why my father slept with Macy Vanderbilt. I know why I was given up. But your father ruined everything. I trusted him at first. I thought he was on my side. But he's not. He wasn't. He used me, and now it's time for him to know what it means to be used. His precious daughter will pay for his sins."

"What are you talking about?" I asked him with a frown, my heart racing.

"He's talking about the fact that Oliver was in love with Jeremiah," Blake spoke up, and my jaw nearly dropped to the floor as I looked at him in shock.

"What?" My eyes nearly popped open. "What are you saying?"

"Oliver was in love with Jeremiah Bradley," Blake said, and the only one who didn't look shocked was Steve. Jakob stepped forward, and I watched as he took his mask off.

"Are you sure?" Jakob said, and Blake nodded.

"Nick caught them in bed together," he said, his face a blank slate, even though he was telling us the most salacious news of the investigation.

"In bed?" I screeched. "Jeremiah and Oliver were in a relationship, or were they just having sex?"

"They were in love!" Steve shouted, and we all jumped. "*That* is why Jeremiah treated me like his own son. I was the son of the man he loved. Oliver wanted them to be a family. But your father ruined it, Bianca. Your father ruined everything."

"Should we go into another room? Or find somewhere private?" I said quietly as I saw a couple looking at us with curious eyes. "We're drawing attention to ourselves," I said and looked at Jakob, my eyes darting to Steve and then back to him, hoping he was understanding the message I was trying to convey, that Steve was unbalanced and this wasn't a good place for us to be hashing anything out.

"We're not going anywhere," Steve snarled, his eyes manic as he gazed at me. "You're not going to ruin this for me, like your father ruined my life." His voice rose again. "I don't care how embarrassed you get."

"That's not quite true, you know," Blake interjected, looking at Steve with narrowed eyes. "It's true that Oliver was in love with Jeremiah. And it's true that he wanted them to be together. He slept with Macy to show Jeremiah that Macy wasn't faithful. He had hoped that Jeremiah would leave Macy and be with him instead. He wanted Jeremiah to come out of the closet and admit their love to the world."

"My father was gay?" Jakob said softly. He had a glazed look on his face and was obviously struggling to process this revelation.

"Penny thinks he was bisexual," Blake said, and it was then I realized that he must have been in contact with Penny again. I wondered why she'd been able to open up to him when she hadn't wanted to open up completely to me and Jakob. As if Blake could read my mind, he looked at me sheepishly. "I was going to tell you what I'd found out right away, but I forgot with so much stuff going on."

"That's okay." I could barely keep everything straight myself.

"She's pretty sure that Jeremiah didn't love Oliver," he continued. "He was using Oliver so that he could get what he wanted from him, just like he used everyone else. But Oliver was so impressionable. He fell for Jeremiah the first moment he met him. He became his staunchest supporter, his number one fan. He worshipped him. He loved him as he'd never loved anyone." He looked at Steve sympathetically.

"How do you know this?" I asked him softly.

"Penny sent me an e-mail. It contained copies of letters that Oliver had sent her from school. Oliver was a prolific writer, and his sister was the only one who knew he was gay. She was the only one he could confide in," Blake said matter-of-factly, but I could see from the way he was staring at me that there was something he wasn't telling me. Something he didn't want Steve to know. Only I had no idea what it was.

"That's what she tried to blackmail Jeremiah with, isn't it?" I said thoughtfully. "That's why she asked for a million dollars all those years ago. To keep her mouth shut. It had nothing to do with Steve being in a foster home or being Jeremiah's long-lost son. It was about his affair with Oliver. That's what he'd do anything to keep secret."

"Yeah." Blake nodded. "She said she realized after Oliver's death that he'd been used. She said that the second-to-last letter she received from Oliver told her that Nick had walked in on him and Jeremiah in bed. He'd been shocked at first, but then happy because he thought it would be a reason for them to come out, maybe live a happier and more honest life. But Jeremiah was angry and insisted he was going to do no such thing. He said that he was going to pay Nick to keep quiet. He'd been confident Nick would take the money because he was still grieving over his wife's death."

"My dad would never do that." I shook my head, knowing in my heart that my dad would never accept a bribe. He had been a good man. I truly believed that. Whatever had happened all those years ago had been a setup. And my father had paid for it with the loss of his wife and his own life.

"No, he didn't." Blake nodded. "He didn't accept any money. He wasn't trying to hurt your father, Steve."

"He stole my father's inventions and passed them off as his," Steve shouted. "And then he ruined my father's relationship. And then, then he said I needed to stay away from Bianca. As if I wasn't good enough for her. I'm good enough. I'll show him I'm good enough."

"What are you talking about, Steve? Calm down." Blake touched his shoulder. "No one has said you're not good enough."

"He's *not* good enough," Jakob spat out, and put his arm around me. "Go back to the loony bin, Steve."

"Jakob!" I gasped, and saw Blake's eyes widen in fear as Steve's face grew angrier. Jakob had said the absolute worst thing he could have said in that moment.

"Sing a song of sixpence," Steve said as he glared at Jakob.

"What?" Jakob's voice was harsh. "What are you talking about?"

"Humpty Dumpty sat on the wall," Steve said, and Jakob, Blake, and I looked at one another. I could feel my skin growing clammy. Steve was even more unbalanced than I'd thought.

"If you're not going to tell us why we're here, or introduce us to whoever it is you want us to meet, then we're going to leave." Jakob drew me to him protectively

"No!" Steve shouted adamantly. "Mary had a little lamb."

"Yes, she did," I said, and touched his hand. "Its fleece was white as snow," I said with a smile, though inside I felt like crying. I didn't understand what was going on, but I knew that I had to try and reach Steve in some way. Try and show him that I understood where he was coming from, and this was the only way I could think of in the moment.

"You could love me, couldn't you?" His eyes glazed over as he looked down at my hand on his. "You could love me with all your heart?"

"You are deserving of love, Steve," I said carefully. I didn't want to lie to him. I wouldn't do that. Not about love. He'd been hurt enough in his life. I couldn't toy with his emotions and make him think that there was that possibility. At least not now. Not unless he pushed me to and I had no other option.

"So was my father." He nodded. "All I want is love. All I need is love."

"And you deserve love."

"Steve, you need to understand that we're here to help you." Blake spoke up again. "Your father was a good man.

Jeremiah should have proven his love to him if he loved him, but he didn't. You can't blame anyone but Jeremiah for what happened." Blake's voice was increasingly urgent, and I could see that he was worried. What was he hiding?

"How do you know so much?" Steve looked at him and frowned. "No one knew they were gay. Only me and Aunty Penny. No one else knew."

"We spoke to Aunty Penny," I said to Steve. "She sent Blake some e-mails, remember?"

"She's gone." Steve looked sad as he stared at me. "She went to France."

"She can send e-mails from France, Steve."

"She's gone to Paris." He looked at Blake. "Do you speak French?"

"*Je ne parle pas français,*" Blake said, and I wanted to groan. Now was not the time for him to play smart.

Steve frowned at Blake and turned to me. "She asked me if I wanted to go with her. She said I could have a good life in France. We'd be family."

"Why didn't you go with her?"

"Because I haven't gotten what I want yet," he said matter-of-factly.

"What do you want?" I asked him softly, trying to let him know that I cared. Maybe, just maybe, he would be on our side if he thought we legitimately cared about him.

"You." He spoke the word so softly that I nearly didn't hear him. His eyes softened as he looked me over, and I stifled a shudder as his fingers stroked my arm. "I want you, Bianca."

"Well, you're not going to have her," Jakob said, and moved so that he was between us. Steve's arm dropped to the side, and he glared at Jakob. "She's mine."

"If it had been just me and her on the island, it would have been us. There would have been no you." Steve's hatred for Jakob was written all over his face.

"No, Steve," I said, but then stopped as I felt Jakob's hand on my lower back.

"Who do you want us to meet?" Jakob said. "Is my father still alive?"

Steve looked at him and laughed. His laughter grew more and more hysterical until he was practically gasping for breath, and if it weren't for the fact that he kept his eyes pinned on us the whole time, I would have fled. As it was, I didn't trust that Steve wouldn't pull a knife if we tried to run. I could feel all eyes on us in our immediate vicinity. Steve had drawn a lot of unwanted attention to our group, and I could see a man approaching us.

"Come with me," Steve said abruptly as he eyed the man. Stepping directly in front of him, he barked, "Go away," in a tone that made the man do an abrupt about-face. Guess there'd be no help from that quarter. He nodded to me and Jakob. "We have to go," he said, all traces of laughter gone from his voice, and then he looked at Blake. "Not you, though. You can't come."

"Okay." Blake looked upset, but he didn't challenge Steve. Who knew what he would do in this erratic emotional state?

Steve turned to me and Jakob. "Put on your masks, and let's go."

"Where's Rosie?" I asked him, surprised that I hadn't seen her yet. "Where is Rosie and where is David?"

"They're waiting for me to tell them you're here," Steve said, and I watched as he pulled out his phone. "Let's go." He turned his back, presumably to conceal his text to Rosie and David, but I couldn't see for sure.

"What do you think?" I whispered to Jakob, but I could see him staring at something on the other side of the room very intently. "Jakob." I grabbed his arm. "What should we do?"

"I don't think we have a choice," he said quickly, still staring across the dance floor. "Blake, I need you to do me a favor." He handed Blake a card. "Call this number if you don't see us in two hours."

"And tell them what?"

"They'll know what to do."

"What are you three whispering about?" Steve's eyes looked beady as he turned around to face us again.

"Nothing." Jakob grabbed my arm. "We're coming with you now, Steve. We trust you and know that you won't do anything to harm us."

"I'm not the one you have to worry about," Steve said with a small smile, and then he gazed at me, his eyes looking almost apologetic. "I'm sorry, Bianca. I, more than anyone, understand what you're going through. I, more than anyone, know what it's like to have a father that has let you down."

"What are you talking about?" I said, but he just turned around and walked away. Jakob and I followed behind him, and I saw Jakob's eyes narrow as he gazed at someone across the room. I stopped still for a second as I thought I recognized Larry. But why would Larry be here? Wasn't he in jail? My heart thudded, and I banished the thought from my mind. I wasn't sure what was going to happen, or how this was going to end. But there was one thing I knew for certain—no matter what happened, Jakob would be by my side. And we'd do whatever we had to so we could both make it out of this victorious.

twelve

"What are you thinking right now?" I asked quietly as we waited in a small dark room. There was one very dim light on in the corner that kept flickering, and the setting felt like the opening of a horror movie, just waiting for the arrival of a vengeful ghost. I was starting to feel panicky. "Do you think we were set up? Do you think Steve is coming back?" I kept mumbling to Jakob as I stared at the closed door. I was starting to feel claustrophobic. "And who did you see in the ballroom as we were walking out?"

"I think Steve is crazy." Jakob sighed. "And perhaps we are too, for coming in here with him. However, I think Steve is the key to this whole mess."

"You do?" I made a face.

"Yes, Steve." Jakob nodded. "He's unbalanced, but he's

not dumb, Bianca. I think he's been playing all sides for a long time now."

"I guess that's true." I nodded. "But whose side is he on? Larry's?"

"I don't know." Jakob shrugged. "And I don't know if I saw anyone in the ballroom. I thought I saw Larry, but I'm not sure."

"He can't have gotten out of jail, already, can he?"

"I don't know," Jakob said, and sighed. "I'm sorry, Bianca. I wish I knew what to say."

"Should we leave?" I said softly. "I don't think the door's locked."

"We've come this far, there's no point in leaving now." He shook his head. "Let's wait." He grabbed my hand, and we stood there in the dark room holding hands and waiting. The only sound in the room was that of our labored breathing. I shifted closer to him as I heard a loud creak in the corner of the room. Finally I'd had enough of the silence and spoke.

"What are you thinking right now?" I asked him, needing to hear his voice.

"I'm thinking about my mom," Jakob said softly. "I'm thinking about what she would say about us being in this situation."

"What would she say?" I said, and gasped as the dim light went out, plunging us into total darkness. I felt Jakob grabbing my arm and pulling me closer to him. "What just happened?" I said as my heart started racing. Why had I been so stupid as to believe Steve and Rosie could be trusted for even a second? My skin felt cold, and my throat felt heavy as tears built up in my eyes. "Maybe Blake will come," I mumbled, but I knew that even he couldn't save us in this moment. If anything, he'd be walking into the trap with us.

"It's okay, Bianca. The bulb just went out. I'm here. I'll protect you." He rubbed my back, and I tried to concentrate on breathing in and out to control my nerves. "Before my mother died, she handed me a poem on a piece of paper. It was a poem that wasn't in her notebook." Jakob's voice cracked as he continued speaking. "She handed it to me and she told me to always keep it close to my heart. To read the words and to live my life according to what it said. She said the worst thing in life is to die with more regrets than not." He rubbed the top of my head, and his voice was soft as he spoke. "I want to recite it to you. I want us to think about my mother's words as we stand here. We're not waiting in vain, Bianca. We're here for a reason. We're here with a purpose. That's all that matters."

"I know." My voice sounded as squeaky as a mouse's. "I'm just glad that I'm here with you."

"Bianca, you don't know how much it means to hear you say that." His voice was gruff. "I know we got off to an inauspicious start, but I've felt from the beginning of this journey that there was a deeper purpose to our meeting. And there was. It was for me to find you." He pulled me toward him, and I felt his lips pressing down on the top of my head softly.

He caressed me with his lips and fingers as my body shook slightly. "I'm not one of those guys who's full of romance and strawberries. I don't always have flowery words or gifts, but I want you to know that this life, this love of ours, it's all I could have ever asked for. It's everything that I wanted that I didn't even know existed. You're the reason my heart is beating right now. You're my everything. We'll get through this, whatever this is. We'll get through it because we have each other."

"You know just what to say when I need you to say it." I reached up, pulled his face down, and gave him a deep kiss. "I wouldn't have chosen anyone other than you," I said against his lips as I pulled back.

"I know." His voice was soft as he faced me, and even though I couldn't really see more than the outline of his face in the dark room, I could feel that his eyes were burning a fire directly into my soul. I stood there staring back at him, and even though our eyes weren't meeting and focusing on each other, I knew we were staring at each other.

"Let me hear your mom's poem," I said softly, knowing how much her words meant to him and loving that he felt connected enough to me to share them.

Jakob started reciting his mother's poem, and his voice filled the room with strength and warmth. "'In the last minute of the last hour on earth, there will be three things I'll regret.'" I closed my eyes, even though the room was dark. I didn't want to concentrate on the dark unknown of the room. I wanted to focus on his voice and the poem and only those two things. "'I'll regret not telling you I loved you. I'll regret not getting to spend another minute with you. And I'll regret not saying no.'" Jakob's voice was heavy, and he paused as we heard a door open behind us. However, he didn't stop talking, and we didn't look around. This was our moment and even though I knew we both wanted to know who was with us, our being in this moment and seeing it through was more important. We were more important than everything else going on around us. "'In the last minute of the last hour on earth, there will be three things I won't regret,'" he said. "'I won't regret meeting you—'"

"'I won't regret loving you, and I'll never regret giving you my heart.'" A familiar voice completed the line. I felt Jakob freeze next to me, and as my eyes popped open, I let go of Jakob's hands and walked toward the door.

"Is it—?" I said, my heart racing as I felt my way toward the voice. The light suddenly came back on, and I stood there squinting in the brightness. I took a step backward as I gazed at the man in the doorway—and suddenly tears poured from my eyes. I couldn't stop them, and I couldn't even think as I just stood there, my body frozen like a statue.

"Bianca." He stepped toward me, his face looking older than I remembered.

"Dad?" I said, and I heard Jakob gasp.

"'In the last minute of the last hour on earth, there will be three things I'll regret.'" My dad continued Jakob's mom's poem as he stared at me, but as he went on the words seemed to change to a confession. "I'll regret not telling you I loved you every single day. I'll regret not getting to spend another minute with you even when my heart is crying out for you. And I'll regret not saying no to Jeremiah Bradley. In the last minute of the last hour on earth, there will be three things I won't regret. I won't regret meeting your mother and having you. I won't regret loving you with all my heart . . . and I'll never regret having to pretend I was dead to save your life." He stopped and held his arms open to me. "Come to me, my darling Bianca. Come to your dear old dad."

"Dad!" I said, crying out as I rushed into his arms. My brain was racing, and all I could think was, *My dad's still alive? My dad's still alive?* I heard Jakob's footsteps behind us, and I pulled back so that I could introduce Jakob to my dad, but then Steve and Rosie walked into the room and slammed the door.

"Well, look who we have here," Rosie said with a twist of her lips. "A dirty slut, a dirty slut's sluttier boyfriend, and a dirty slut's dad."

"Roma," Jakob's voice was harsh. "Enough."

"Enough?" She tilted her head back and started laughing. "Enough? Oh, no, dear Jakob. We're just getting started."

thirteen

"Dad, you're alive?" I stepped back from him, my voice showing my deep hurt. "What's going on?"

"Bianca." His eyes looked at me sadly, his face but a shadow of what I remembered. "I did it for you."

"Did what for me, Dad?" My voice grew louder. "Pretended you were dead?"

"Guess he won't win Dad of the Century after all," Rosie said with a sneer.

"What the fuck is your problem?" I screamed at her, finally having enough of her snarky comments. "I thought you were my best friend!"

"I'm a good actress, I suppose."

"You're a bitch."

"Why? Because I'm a better actress than you are a writer?"

she snarled at me. "You with your shitty-ass articles about shitty-ass movies."

"You're the one who told me about the job." My voice showed my hurt, and I felt my dad rubbing my back, and I pushed his hand off me.

"Because you were always going on about movies. Movies, movies, movies. How blind can you be?" Rosie looked at me in disgust. "There's a whole world out there, a whole world of money and fame and fortune, and you're too busy thinking about history and bloody movies." Her eyes were slits as she gazed at me. "Pathetic."

"You hate me because I enjoy movies?"

"I don't hate you." She laughed. "I'd have to care about you to hate you. I can't stand your pity parties. Oh, pity me, my dad died. Oh, pity me, I need to make money. Oh, pity me, I got kidnapped and I fucked my kidnapper. Shit, have some self-respect."

I looked down at the ground, embarrassed to be having this conversation in front of Jakob and my dad, and I could feel the tears falling silently from my eyes. It was all too much. I didn't even know where to look. I didn't want to look at my dad or Jakob. And I couldn't stand to even look at Rosie anymore. So I looked at Steve, and I was struck by the uncomfortable look on his face. His eyes met mine, and I could see that he felt sorry for me. In all his craziness, there was a very real possibility that Steve really did have feelings for me.

"Why are we here, Steve?" I asked him.

"Your dad wanted to see you," he said, his eyes never leaving mine. "He said it was time."

"You knew my dad was alive? This whole time?"

"Do you remember when I told you that there weren't many things I wouldn't do to have a girlfriend like you?" he asked as he caressed my cheek, his eyes lightening.

"No." I shook my head and tried not to push him away from me.

"On the island. That day we spoke. Remember?" He looked agitated.

"Oh, vaguely," I said, my heart racing.

"Steve, is this all really necessary?" Rosie said, annoyed. "Have you called David? Where is he? I thought he was meeting us in here?"

"Shut up!" Steve shouted, and looked at Rosie. "Just shut up."

"What?" She frowned. "Who do you think you're talking to?"

"Shut up," he said again, this time pulling a gun out of his waistband and pointing it at her. "Open your mouth again, and I'll shoot you."

"Steve." Rosie looked panicked. "What's going on?"

"You think you're in charge? You think you can play me?" he screamed. "No one plays me!"

"Steve, I don't know what they've been telling you. You know I'm on your side."

"No, you're not." His eyes glazed over, and he looked angry. "I know what you and your father did. I know. I know. I know."

"Steve . . . ," she said again, but this time her voice trailed off. She ran to the door and tried to open it, but it was locked. "Let me out, Steve. Let me go get David. Please let me out."

"I won't let you go." He shook his head and turned back to me. I stood there not knowing if his last words had been to me or to Rosie.

"Steve, let Bianca and Rosie go," Jakob said as he moved to stand next to me.

"Don't move another inch." Steve pointed the gun at Jakob. "Or I'll shoot." He started laughing again then, and my stomach dropped. "Bianca, I tried to tell you, didn't I?"

"Tell me what?"

"I tried to warn you that I was the good guy. I am the good guy. I'm working with your dad. I helped your dad. I did this. I did this all."

"Did what?" I turned to my dad. "What's going on, Dad?"

"Steve worked for the company." His voice sounded sad, and he looked at me with a pleading expression. "He was very close with Jeremiah Bradley."

"I was his intern. His trusted intern," Steve said. "I was special."

"Yes," my dad said carefully, and slowly moved toward

me. His dark hair had grayed completely, and he looked like a much older version of himself. It was so weird standing here, staring at him. Watching him talk. Staring into his eyes. My dad. My dead dad. It was surreal, and as much as I loved him, I also hated him. I hated him for making me think he was dead. I hated him for lying to me.

"I don't understand." I rubbed my forehead.

"I thought I was special." Steve's voice dropped, and he banged his fist against the wall. "I grew up moving from foster home to foster home. Then one day, I get this opportunity out of the blue. I didn't even know why at first. I didn't even know. I had parents. I had a brother. I could have had a real life. A real shot."

"I didn't know that Steve was Oliver's son. None of us did," my father continued, rubbing his temples. "I should have known, of course. I should have known, but I was so caught up in my pain at losing your mother. Everything was so confusing to me." He looked at Jakob. "And I'd been living with guilt for a long time over your mother."

"You loved her?" I asked him, my heart stopping.

"As a friend," he said softly. "Only as a friend. I knew she liked me. I knew that I was walking a fine line between the two women." He sighed. "I wasn't perfect." He hung his head for a few seconds before continuing. "I didn't really realize how deep things had been, not just for me, but for everyone." He looked at Steve. "I'm sorry that it came to this."

"Penny tried to look out for me," Steve said. "Aunty

Penny knew about me. She knew that I'd been given up, but one day she saw me and she just knew I was her nephew. She used to come to Bradley Inc. to speak to Jeremiah. Harass him, you could say." He laughed. "And one day she recognized me. I used to work a lot with Larry. She recognized me. I looked like my dad, you see. She realized it was me. She took me to the side. She made me promise not to say anything." He looked young and confused in that moment. "I didn't really understand. She didn't tell me much. Just that my dad had worked for the company and that he'd died. She found out I used to work a lot with Larry and that was when she started to get to know him, flirt with him, play him. She did that for me. And she told me that Dad's best friend had been a guy called Nick London. So I got to know him."

"I didn't realize at first." My dad sighed. "It should have been clear as day, because Steve looked so much like a young Oliver, but all I could think about was Angelina. I didn't really know the web I was in. I didn't know." He looked at me. "I failed you and your mom, Bianca, and I'm sorry."

"I thought Nick could tell me about my dad, so I asked him about the women Oliver had dated. I wanted to know who my mom was," Steve continued, almost sounding rational, almost making me feel more compassion toward him than hate.

"I didn't know why he was asking. Oliver was gay," my

dad said softly. "He had no girlfriends that I knew of." He shook his head. "Jeremiah had been sleeping with him, leading him on. Trying to use him to ruin me. I knew that, but I didn't want to tell Steve that. I didn't want to spread rumors. That wasn't my place."

"Why was Jeremiah trying to ruin you, Dad?" I said softly. "Because of you and Mom?"

"I don't really know why he wanted to ruin my life. I didn't know he was so depraved. At least at the time I never would have believed he would have been capable of doing the things that he did." My dad looked sad. "I don't know that there was a real reason. I mean, yes, superficially Jeremiah wanted to ruin me because he felt slighted that your darling mother chose me. But the thing is, he only started dating your mother once he realized I was interested in her. So it wasn't as if I took someone he loved. He always wanted to have something over me. I just didn't realize it until it was too late."

"So he was jealous of you?" I asked, confused.

"No, it wasn't even that. Jeremiah just liked to play games. With everyone. He had a sadistic side. He thought he was some sort of god." My dad looked tired as he spoke, and I just wanted to run into his arms and hold him close.

"But what was his purpose in doing all of this?" I asked, my voice sounding like I was whining. "What did he want from it all?"

"He wanted to prove he was the most powerful man in

the world." My father's eyes crinkled as he reached out and touched the top of my head. "My darling Bianca. You look so much like your mother. I was scared I'd never see you again."

"I can't believe you left me, Dad. I can't believe you made me think you were dead."

"It was the only way." He sighed. "I didn't want to leave, but once Jeremiah threatened you, I knew you were in danger."

"He threatened me?"

"My father was going to harm Bianca?" Jakob looked confused. "Why?"

"I don't know. Maybe he thought Steve and I were becoming too close. Maybe he thought I was going to reveal things he didn't want revealed. Maybe he just wanted to make sure that I paid once again for going against him. At least that's what I thought when Steve told me I should leave town."

"Steve told you that?" I was surprised and looked at Steve. "Why?"

"He was my friend," Steve said simply. "I trusted him. He told me things about my dad. He told me that my dad had invented the patents and that he wasn't the one that had created the products. He told me he was trying to get the inventions out of his name. He said it wasn't right. He said that there were people in the company who had tried to destroy his name."

"I didn't realize they were also trying to destroy my family," Nick said. "I didn't realize that Angelina's death wasn't an accident."

"She didn't cheat with Jeremiah, did she, Dad?" My breath caught. "She didn't have an affair?"

"No." He shook his head. "Your mother never liked Jeremiah. She loved me. She was always true to me. It was I who failed her."

"What?" I looked at him in horror. "Please, Dad, tell me that's not true."

"I slept with Joanie." He nodded and looked down in shame. "I slept with Jakob's mother." He looked at Jakob. "I'm sorry. I was so sorry. She loved me so much. I was her friend. And I kind of dropped her when Angelina and I got together." He looked back at me. "Your mother was jealous of our friendship, but Joanie and I got each other. I never loved her, not in that way. I just needed someone to talk to. And one night, it happened."

"Because these things just happen, right?" Rosie's voice was sharp as she spoke up. I looked over at her and studied her face, wondering if she really was as cold and callous inside as she sounded.

"It shouldn't have happened," my dad answered her, rubbing his eyes. When he looked back at me I could see his pained expression. "It was only the one night. I told your mom right away. She was heartbroken. She went to see Joanie. They argued. It was bad—so bad. I hurt them both.

And then your mother died"—his voice cracked—"in a car accident, and I was devastated. I blamed myself. She'd been crying that day. I thought she'd been crying so hard she was distracted. I withdrew into myself. Nothing was important anymore." His voice trailed off. "Don't hate me, Bianca."

"So my father killed your wife?" Jakob's voice was a monotone, and I turned to see how he was taking the news of what had happened. His eyes looked into mine, and all I saw was sympathy. My heart soared that he wasn't blaming me.

"No, I don't think it was your dad." My dad chewed his lower lip. "At the time, I thought it was an accident. And then I did think it was your dad. But, it isn't your dad that I'm worried about now."

"Then who?" Jakob said with a frown. I knew he was as confused and overwhelmed as I.

"Larry," my father said softly. "Larry was the one to worry about. It was always Larry."

"What are you talking about?" Rosie said, her voice sharp. "My dad didn't do anything. He's an innocent victim here. He only got involved to right the wrongs that were done to him. He was always used and left behind." Her face was twisted. "Stop trying to make yourself the victim. This is all because of you and Jeremiah and your games. You hurt people. You're the ones responsible for what has gone on here. My dad is a good man."

"No, he's not." My father shook his head. "I know it. And Steve knows it, don't you, Steve?"

"I don't know." His eyes were blank. "I don't know anymore. You lied to me."

"Steve, I didn't lie to you."

"Then why isn't she with me? Why doesn't she love me?" He cocked his gun up in the air and started pacing back and forth. "You said she would love me."

"I can't help who my daughter falls in love with," my father said softly as he moved closer to me. "There will be another woman for you, Steve."

"I don't want another woman. I want Bianca."

"You don't even know me, Steve. You don't want me. You don't love me," I pleaded with him. "Please just let us go."

"From the first time I saw your photograph on your father's desk, I knew," he said as he gazed at me lovingly. "And then you wrote him that note, and my heart broke into a thousand pieces, for I knew you were the one."

"What note?" I frowned.

"The note where you told him he was the best dad ever." He closed his eyes, and he seemed to fall into a trance. "You told him that he was the best dad ever and that you loved him more than words could say. You told him that if you could meet a man like him, you'd be blessed."

"I did?" I frowned and looked at my dad. "What note was this?"

"It was a Father's Day card you gave me." My dad's face blanched. "I had it on my desk at work, next to your photo."

"That's why I gave you all the clues in the notes," Steve said lovingly. "I knew you would appreciate them. I knew you would see the feelings behind the notes."

"You left me all the notes?" I said, shocked. "I thought it was Larry."

"Larry?" Steve scoffed. "Of course it wasn't Larry; it was me. I tried to help you, Bianca. I tried to let you know the truth without going against your father's wishes. I even called you on your father's phone."

"That was you?" I thought back to the day that the fake policeman broke into my house. "You weren't the policeman though."

"No, that was my friend Trevor," Steve said. "I was the one who called you though. You were making too many silly mistakes; letting strangers into your house and trusting people. I wanted you to be careful. I wanted you to be wary of strangers."

"Be careful of those who seek to help you. They may do more harm than good," I said as I recalled the words he'd spoken into the phone.

"You remember!" His eyes lit up, and he walked toward me. "I knew you'd remember. I knew you'd get it."

"You were warning me about David?"

"David and Jakob." His voice dropped. "And Rosie. They were all in it together, colluding to bring you down and get revenge. They didn't know your dad was alive or that I'd told them Larry planned to get rid of him."

"I thought you said Jeremiah was trying to get rid of us?"

I said softly, and stepped closer to him. I cocked my head to the side trying to get Jakob and my father to move to the side of the room. I wanted to make Steve feel like we were the only two people here, to think only of me. Maybe then I could get him to open the door. Maybe then I could get us all out of here.

"Jeremiah didn't care about anyone. Only himself." Steve shook his head. "But he wasn't violent."

"And he had a conscience," Jakob spoke up, his eyes burning into mine. I could tell that he wanted to approach Steve, and my eyes issued him a warning to stay back.

"Jeremiah Bradley didn't have a conscience," Rosie snapped. "He used everyone to make money and then he dropped them. He was selfish and killed everyone who got in his way."

"He had a conscience," Jakob said again, and looked at me. "Think about it. He hired Steve as an intern. I don't think it was to keep him from revealing anything. Steve didn't have anything to reveal. He did that because he felt guilty about what he did to Oliver. Just like with me. He gave my mom money, not because he cared about her well-being, but because I was his son and he wanted to provide. He had a sense of duty to those around him. A perverted sense of duty, perhaps, but I don't think he was a murderer."

"You're a smart man." My father looked at Jakob with respect. "All these years, I was the smartest one in the group, or so I thought, but I was fooled. I didn't figure it out until recently."

"Figure what out?" I asked, confused. "What are you guys talking about? Are you trying to say that Jeremiah wasn't so evil after all?"

"Oh, he was evil, all right," my father said quietly. "He just wasn't a killer."

"So who, then?" My voice trailed off as I realized the answer. It had been there all along. Under my nose. "Larry?" I said softly, and looked at Rosie. "It was Larry, wasn't it?"

"Shut up, you stupid bitch!" Rosie screamed at me. Her eyes were wild, but I could see that she was starting to realize what we were saying was true. "He would never do that," she said, but this time her voice wasn't so confident. I recognized the look of pain and confusion on her face as she waited for my dad's answer. It was the same way I'd felt when I'd realized that my dad hadn't been the complete innocent that I'd thought him to be.

"I don't know what happened to you, Rosie." My father looked at her. "I didn't even know you were Brigitta's daughter until I met up with her one day and she showed me photographs of you. Then I realized you were the same girl who was my Bianca's best friend. At first I thought nothing of it, but then I began to realize that maybe you had a hidden agenda. Especially after your mother told me you'd stopped talking to her after you'd become close with your dad."

"She didn't understand him!" she cried out. "She didn't

appreciate his greatness. No one did. Everyone took advantage of him. He needed me. I was the only one who hadn't forsaken him. I had to help him. I had to show him that he had someone who loved him."

"He had his wife," Jakob said, and she glared at him.

"That woman was not his wife. That woman was a drain on him."

"So you befriended me to keep an eye on me?" I asked her. "Help me to understand, Rosie. Was our whole friendship fake?" I bit my lower lip as I thought about all the years we'd spent together laughing, shopping, gossiping. How could all of it have been a lie?

"Bianca, why do you think I had to go on so many business trips? Why do you think I had to drink so much when I was around you? You are the most infantile, annoying—"

"Do not talk to Bianca like that!" Steve pointed the gun at Rosie, and she screamed.

"Get that thing away from me. David will be looking for me, and when he finds us, he'll kill you."

"David?" Steve said, and laughed hysterically.

I looked at my dad then, still needing more answers. "So are you saying Larry was the one behind everything?"

My dad nodded. "Larry and I met in college. He was Jeremiah's friend from high school. He was never very friendly, but I thought he was just a snob. I was wrong. Larry was fiercely jealous of Jeremiah, and he hated that he made friends so quickly and easily. Larry hated having to take a backseat to

Jeremiah. He wanted to be number one. He wanted everyone to know that he was rich and smart and brilliant. All of the major ideas were Jeremiah's, but Larry was the one who carried them all out. Larry fixed problems. Even problems that Jeremiah didn't know he had." My father sighed. "I wish I'd paid more attention to him. I wish I'd seen the signs."

"We were all fooled," Jakob spoke up. "I had no idea that Larry had this other side to him. I had no idea that he even knew what was really going on. He's smart, I'll give him that. Manipulative and smart. He made me and David think it was our plan to kidnap Bianca. He made it seem like he was trying to help us get to the truth. He's the one who told me about Nick and Angelina breaking my mom's heart. He sowed the seeds and then waited for them to germinate. He was the one out for revenge, and he used us to get it. He played us all."

"But why?" I let out an exasperated sigh. "What did he hope to get from all of this?"

"He wanted to walk away with the company," my father said. "His plan was for him and Rosie to own Bradley Incorporated. That's why she's dating David. They're covering all their bases."

"That's why they gave me the shares, isn't it? Larry wanted me to go down for fraud." I looked over at Rosie, but she didn't react. She just stood there with a blank face.

"Yes." My father nodded. "He tried to do the same thing to me. When he put the patents in my name, I asked him what was going on. He said Jeremiah thought it was the smart thing to do. I didn't really know what to say, but Oliver and Jeremiah both agreed, so I went along with it. By the time I realized that Jeremiah was still angry at me for stealing Angelina, it was too late. The patents were already in my name, and Oliver had proof that he was the inventor and designer. I was going to Jeremiah's apartment that day to tell him that I wanted to come clean and that I didn't want to be a part of the company anymore. And then I walked in on him and Oliver, in bed."

"My father really loved Jeremiah. That's what Penny told me," Steve interrupted my dad. "He would have done anything for him."

"Yes." My dad nodded. "I should have seen the signs when I was younger. Oliver was so protective of Jeremiah, even from the beginning, but I was so focused on Angelina. I loved her so much that nothing else was important after we got together."

I wanted to ask him why he cheated on her, then, if he'd loved her so much. But now wasn't the time or the place, and I didn't want to hurt Jakob. It was a weird situation to be in—I was in love with the son of the woman my father had had an affair with. Did it make it better that she had loved him? Had my dad been the love of Jakob's mom's life? Knowing that her poems were about him made me feel funny, awkward even. I wondered how Jakob felt. I couldn't tell anything from his face. He didn't even look shocked. Or scared. Or nervous. He looked apathetic, except when he met my eyes. Then he seemed passionate and determined. He gave me a small secret smile as if to tell me he loved me and to stay strong. It was a miracle that I hadn't fainted when my father had walked into the room. I guess I was growing stronger day by day.

"That's what love is," Steve said, his voice suddenly energized. "Love is being there and doing whatever you can to be with the one you love." All of a sudden he grabbed my arm and pulled me to the door.

"What are you doing?" I squeaked.

"Let go of her!" Jakob ran toward us, and then everything seemed to happen in a blur. All I heard was a bang from Steve's gun and my own voice screaming. Jakob fell to the ground. Then Steve fumbled with the door as I started crying. Rosie stood in the corner of the room, her eyes wide and her face white. I wasn't sure if I imagined it or not, but I thought she mouthed *sorry* to me.

"Steve, let Bianca go. Let her come with me," my father said softly as he walked toward us in slow motion. The room started spinning as I heard another loud bang. I watched as my father fell to the ground, and I tried to push Steve away, but my movements seemed to make no difference. "Jakob!" I screamed. "Dad!" The tears were completely blurring my vision now, and I kicked Steve as hard as I could. He looked at me with murderous eyes, and I saw him pull something out of his pocket.

"Remember, Bianca, this is because I love you," he said as the world went black.

fourteen

I awoke to the feeling of something crawling on my face, and stifled a cry as my eyes adjusted to the dark dingy space. I could see Steve standing in front of me, his eyes focused on my face as he watched me looking around the room. I tried to move my arms and legs, but found they were tightly tied to an uncomfortable chair. My whole body ached as I sat there. I opened my mouth to scream, but nothing came. I felt something on my face again and shook my head. A trail of water slid down my lips and I looked up. The crawling sensation was from drops of water falling from the ceiling.

I looked at Steve again, not knowing what to say. My mind was on Jakob and my dad. Were they okay? Were they dead? The thought of losing them sunk my spirits even further, and my head dropped forward. I heard Steve humming something softly as he walked closer to me. His voice grew louder and louder.

"Hush little baby, don't say a fucking word," he sang in an ominous voice, twisting the lyrics to the old nursery rhyme. His voice was the only sound in the small damp space aside from a low rattling in the corner; I didn't want to know what or who was making that noise. Steve's fingers ran down the side of my cheek, and I kept my expression blank and my eyes downward as I sat there uncomfortably. The room was cold and dark and smelled of mold. I coughed as the mildew filled my lungs, and my body shivered on the old rickety chair I was tied to. I wanted to beg Steve to let me go. I wanted to plead for my life, but I didn't. I didn't even bother trying to scream; no one would hear me. No one would be coming to my rescue now. It was just the two of us. After everything, it had come to this. Me and Steve. Not even Jakob could save me.

Numbly, I thought of Blake. Maybe he could team up with Rosie and come to my rescue. I almost laughed then. Rosie wasn't my friend. She'd never been my friend. She hated me. She'd set me up. She was never coming to save me. And Blake, well, there was nothing he could do by himself. My head dropped forward with fatigue. I just wanted to sleep and forget that any of this had ever happened. I wanted to forget, not because I was scared of this moment or of Steve, but because my heart ached for all the moments of the last week, for the devastating truth that I'd had to accept.

My heart was laden with guilt and regret for the actions that had brought us here. This moment was fate: cold, hard fate, and I knew that there was nothing either of us could say or do to escape the tangled paths of our forefathers. If only my father hadn't met Steve's father. If only he hadn't introduced Oliver to Jeremiah. If only he hadn't dated my mother. If only someone had realized how evil Larry was. But it didn't matter. Not now. And not ever. For there was no way to go back. No way to change the past. And if we changed the past, then there would be no me and Jakob. No true love filling my heart, even as I sat there with pain weighing me down. And I knew that even after everything, I wasn't sure I would have changed a thing.

"I didn't want everything to go like this." Steve held the gun to my head. "You understand that, right? I didn't want to hurt you. I didn't want it to come to this." His voice broke as he spoke, and I nodded my understanding, my throat too constricted to speak.

"A life for a life, right?" His voice sounded broken and raw. "That's what they say, right?" His voice echoed his sorrow. He didn't want to do this, but I knew he thought he had no other option. I couldn't allow myself to look up at him. All I could think was, *Is this how it's all going to end for me? Is this how my story's going to end?*

"He shouldn't have done that to my parents, Bianca." His voice was pained. "He ruined my life."

"I understand," I said softly, my voice cracking as I spoke.

I did understand. I didn't know if I could blame him. "It's not your fault." I took a deep breath and tried to reason with him. "But my father wasn't the one to blame. My father didn't do this. It was Larry."

"You're making this hard for me, Bianca." He sighed and kneeled next to me, moving the gun away from my head. He grabbed my chin and forced me to look at him. His eyes bored into mine, and I could see the regret shining at me. Regret and another emotion I recognized. My heart thudded as I stared back at him. I still had a shot at changing my story. The emotion in his eyes was one I knew well—adoration. He had feelings for me. That was the opening I needed to try to change his mind.

"You don't have to do this," I said softly. "You don't have to go through with it."

"I do," he said, but his voice was unsure as he gazed at me, his eyes scrutinizing my face. "I know what I have to do, but I wanted to make this last moment special. I wanted it to just be you and me, just once. The two of us together—alone. Without Rosie or Jakob or even your dad." He sounded wistful as he spoke. "So yes, I have to do this, but at least when I do, it will be special. Something the both of us will share and never forget." He laughed then. "Though I suppose in death, one will forget anyway."

"Steve," I said, my voice cracking as I swallowed hard. "Don't do this."

"I have to."

"No. If you do, we can't be together." I nearly choked

on the words, but I knew I had to say them. It was my only chance.

"You would want to be with me?" He froze. "After all this?"

"Yes." I nodded and made myself smile. "We're meant to be together, don't you see that?"

"It was always you, you know." His fingers touched my leg. "From the first time I saw you, I knew. You're here because your father told me I couldn't have you. He told me that we weren't destined for each other. After all I did for him! After all the lies I told. The secrets I kept. I'm responsible for you still being alive. I'm the one who deserves you. Not Jakob."

"So then don't do this," I pleaded with him. "This doesn't have to be the end for us. This can be the beginning."

"A new beginning?" He spoke softly, his eyes glazing over as he considered what I'd said.

"Maybe this is why everything happened," I said, my voice shaky. "Maybe we're meant to be together. Maybe this was fate's cruel joke on us. Maybe this was the only way."

"Maybe." He nodded and stepped back. My body was trembling as I waited for him to decide what he was going to do next. "You really think we're soul mates?" He stared at my lips, and it took everything in me not to shudder at his gaze. And then suddenly there was a loud bang. I screamed. He fell forward, his head hitting my lap hard, and I screamed again.

"No!" Tears fell from my eyes as a pool of red blood filled my lap. I felt momentary relief that it wasn't me he'd shot, but seeing him like that made me feel sick to my stomach. "No!" I screamed, and looked into his face. What had just happened? I wasn't even sure. Had he shot himself? He gazed at me with a weak smile, the life draining from his face.

"Your father did this to us," he mumbled. "He did this to me."

"No," I whispered, my stomach churning as I felt a wave of arctic coldness fill me. "I'm sorry," I said honestly. This wasn't how it was supposed to end.

"Hush, my little baby, don't say a fucking word," he said again, though this time his voice was but a whisper in the coldness. "This is how it should be."

"Steve?" I shook him as I stared around the room, desperate to find the source of the gunshot. "Steve!"

"We'll be together forever now, Bianca," he mumbled as his eyes fluttered. "There's no getting out of here for either of us. We'll be together forever." And then he stopped speaking, and his body slumped to the floor. I screamed then. I couldn't control myself. I screamed and screamed and screamed until I couldn't scream anymore. And then I started crying. I sobbed until I was hoarse, but no one came for me, and Steve's body remained immobile at my feet.

Then the creaking started up again in the corner. I peered into the darkness and made out a rat scrabbling along the wall. And that shut me up. I sat there staring at the rat, praying that it wouldn't see me. It took a few steps. And then a few more. And then it stopped when it reached Steve's body. I didn't see what it decided to do next because I closed my eyes as soon as I heard the munching. But I knew what was going on. It was impossible not to know. I wasn't dumb, but I wanted to pretend it wasn't happening. And a part of me was pleased that Steve's body was there, so that it wasn't me that the rat was chewing on.

I must have fallen asleep then because I awoke to water falling on my face again. I shook my head and bit my lower lip. My hands were almost completely numb now, and it didn't look like anyone was coming to untie me. I looked at Steve's body again, but I didn't see the rat. I didn't hear him either. That made me pleased at first, but then scared. If I didn't know where it was, that meant it could creep up on me and scare me. It didn't make a difference to me that the thing must have weighed three pounds. It was a rat. And it could gnaw my toes off. I took a couple of deep breaths. I knew I was close to a panic attack. I screamed to let out my pent-up energy, but it didn't help. I shifted in the chair and tried to move my hands, but Steve had done a good job with the rope. I wished Jakob was with me then. He was the rope man. Just like on the island, he would have known what to do to get the rope off my body. My heart ached as I thought about him. *If you can hear me, Jakob, answer me. Send me a sign. Just send me a sign.* I was pleading with him in my head, but I got no answer.

"Please, God, please let him be okay. Please let him be alive. Please." I bit my lower lip and tried to remember the prayers I'd said in church as a child. I wasn't much of a religious person, but I supposed that I, like most holiday Christians, came back to God when I needed him. "Our Father," I said, remembering the Lord's Prayer that we'd said before all of our prayers. The priest at my church had always told us that whenever you wanted something really badly that we should pray and always say the Lord's Prayer before our own personal prayer. I'd never really listened before, but now I was determined to try everything. "Who art in heaven, hallowed be thy name, thy kingdom come, thy will be done, on earth as it is in heaven." My voice choked as I kept speaking. "Give us this day our daily bread," I said, and my stomach growled, reminding me of how hungry I was. "And forgive us our trespasses, as we forgive those who trespass against us. Lead us not into temptation, but deliver us from evil, for thine is the kingdom, the power and the glory, forever and ever, amen," I said loudly, my voice growing more and more energetic as I spoke. I felt an odd sense of calm as I sat there and I wondered for a moment if God was going to come down from the heavens himself and untie me from the chair.

"I promise I'll be a good person. I promise I'll never do anything bad again. I'll dedicate my life to you, God, please." I cried as I sat there, but nothing happened. "God, please help me, please make Jakob be okay, and my father. Please. Please help me. I don't want to die in here, God. I don't want to die tied up on a chair, next to a dead crazy man. I don't want a rat to eat my dead corpse. Please, God!" I cried out, and then paused as I heard a noise. Were my prayers being answered already? I sat there in anticipation but realized that the sound that I'd heard was just the rat. He was back.

This was God's answer to me. He'd sent a rat.

I started laughing then, hysterical laughter that reminded me of Steve. Poor, sad Steve. My heart ached for what he'd had to endure. And for what? Two crazy, selfish, power-hungry egomaniacs? How was that fair? How was any of it fair? Such senseless crimes. Such senseless deaths. Too many people had been affected by Larry and Jeremiah. And for what? A childhood rivalry? I sat there thinking about how unfair everything was when I heard a loud banging. I froze suddenly and listened carefully. There was definitely a loud banging coming from somewhere outside the room.

"I'm in here!" I shouted at the top of my lungs. "I'm here!" I kept screaming and screaming. I started to grow excited as the banging continued, growing louder and louder. "I'm in here," I cried again, and when the door burst open, I burst into tears.

"Bianca." Jakob's voice was hoarse as he gazed at me with bloodshot eyes. He was clutching the side of his body and I could see that his white shirt was stained red with blood.

"Jakob!" I gazed at him, my heart bursting with love.

"Oh, Bianca." He ran toward me, and I could see Blake following him into the room. "You're safe. Oh my darling, thank God you're safe."

"Oh, Jakob," I cried out as I stared up into his face. "You truly are a godsend." I started laughing at my joke. Jakob looked at me for a few seconds, confused, but Blake mumbled something about me being in shock as they both started to untie the rope from my wrists and ankles. I continued to laugh as I sat there and watched the rat scurry out of the room. I'd probably made him a believer as well. I'd said a prayer to God and He'd saved us both. It was a pity I hadn't said one for Steve as well.

~

I slept for eighteen hours on a hospital chair. The nurses told me that that was a record. No one had ever slept for more than an hour before. Eighteen hours was unheard of. They'd offered me a bed, but I'd turned them down. I wasn't going to leave Jakob's room, not for love nor money. I'd slept through his surgery, and I was upset with myself for sleeping even when he'd gotten out. I woke up to him staring at me.

"Good sleep?" he'd asked me softly as my eyes fluttered open.

"Yes, you?" I asked, and jumped up, touching his shoulder gingerly. "Are you okay?"

"My shoulder's fine," he joked. "It's my chest that's a little achy."

"They said if he'd shot you a few inches higher, you'd be dead," I said, my voice catching. "He tried to kill you."

"He didn't though," he said, and grabbed my hand. "Do you know about your dad?"

"He died." I nodded, my heart aching. "I don't know how to feel," I said softly. "Does that make me a bad daughter? I feel sad, but I'm not grieving. I think because I grieved for so long before that it doesn't even seem real now."

"You're still in shock," he said. "Come lie with me on the bed."

"I can't get on the bed. You're in pain."

"Come lie with me. I want to hold you," he said, and pulled me up. I settled into the bed and curled into his good side, suddenly feeling warm as his body pressed into mine. "Your father wanted to make sure you were safe. He gave his life for yours."

"He didn't have to die," I said with a sob, and I could feel warm tears springing from my eyes. "It didn't have to happen like this." I grabbed his hand and held it close to me. "And you, how stupid were you to run in front of Steve like that? If anything had happened to you, Jakob, if I'd lost you, I wouldn't have been able to go on. I wouldn't have been able to live the rest of my life."

"Oh, Bianca, I would give my life for yours in an instant."

"I know, and I love you for it." I sighed and closed my eyes, loving the feeling of being warm and safe. "Is it over? What happened to Rosie? Is Larry still in jail? And where's David?"

"Larry is being held by the FBI," Jakob said softly. "He's in federal custody and being prosecuted for insider trading, attempted bribery, extortion, and racketeering. Rosie tried to run off, but they have her in questioning as well."

"How did they get Larry?" I asked, surprised. "He hid his tracks so well."

"David helped us."

"David?" I asked, shocked. "What?"

"After we found out Rosie was Larry's daughter, I knew she was playing us all," he said. "That's why I went to go and see David that day. That video you saw wasn't real," he said, and sighed. "David and I were acting."

"David believed you?"

"He'd been suspicious of Rosie for a while." Jakob nodded. "And of Larry. He said that he knew that something fishy was going on, but he could never figure it out."

"But he hates you," I said with a frown. "Why would he believe you?"

"David doesn't hate anything but having to actually work for a living." Jakob sighed. "He bought into Larry's hype. Larry told him that I was planning on taking the company away from him and that I wasn't to be trusted. He thought I was after all the Bradley money."

"But you did buy the company, right?" I said, my head hurting as I tried to get my mind around everything. "Why did you do that?"

"I did it for you," he said, and his fingers ran up to my

breasts. "I wanted you to own the company that was founded on your father's inventions."

"But they weren't my father's inventions," I said. "They were Oliver's."

"Actually, they were both of theirs," Jakob said. "I had an IP attorney look at all the paperwork. The ideas were Oliver's, but your father helped him build the working prototypes. So technically they're both the inventors."

"So why did he try to get the patents out of his name, then?" I said. "And how did Jeremiah think he could take my dad down that way?"

"Maybe technically your father didn't actually consider himself an inventor." He nodded. "He didn't want the patents in his name because all he was really doing was helping Oliver, but based on the paperwork we've found, he was responsible for some key upgrades to the prototype." He shrugged and looked at me. "It's a gray area. And that's what Larry knew. He knew your father was an honest man, and that was the way to get to him. So that's what Larry told Jeremiah. He knew that Jeremiah wanted to take down your dad, and he knew that your dad did not feel that he was a real coinventor of the inventions. So he played them both," Jakob said softly. "Larry was the guiding force behind everything. He lied to everyone. He was the one who caused your mother's death. And he was the one who was actually responsible for Oliver's death as well, and my father's."

"He killed them all?" My eyes grew wide, and I turned around to face him. I rested my hand on his chest and asked him softly, "Why did he do that?"

"He wanted to be number one," Jakob said, and leaned forward to kiss me. "He felt inferior and wanted to show everyone that he was running the show."

"He was setting us up from the beginning, then?"

"Yup." Jakob nodded. "Only problem is that he didn't count on Steve outwitting him and warning your dad. He didn't count on Steve falling in love with your photograph or getting so crazy."

"His parents' deaths really affected him." I sighed.

"No, it wasn't just that," Jakob said. "Steve saw himself as your savior. That's why he gave you the clues. That's why he turned on me on the island. All this time, Steve has been doing this for you. He wanted to protect you. You were the only one he cared about."

"But he didn't even know me."

"Remember that note that he left you?" Jakob said. "The one we found in the old shack on the island?"

"The one that said, 'Your life may be saved in death'?"

"Yes." He nodded. "That one. He was telling you that he was saving your life by having faked your father's death. He's the one who convinced Larry he'd had the body cremated. He took care of everything."

"I had no idea."

"None of us did."

"That makes me feel ever sadder," I said. "It seems so unfair."

"He was crazy, Bianca." Jakob squeezed my hands. "There was nothing you could have done to help. He was crazy."

"So what's going to happen to Larry and Rosie?"

"I think they'll both go to jail for a long time," Jakob said, and smiled.

"Are you sure? Is there any proof?"

"Loads." He grinned. "Penny kept all of the paperwork that Larry told her to shred. And she recorded all of his cell phone calls."

"What?"

"Crazy, right?" He shook his head in amazement. "Here we were thinking she was doing anything she could to protect her husband, but she was trying to set him up. It had been her plan from the day Oliver died that she was going to make Larry pay for his role in influencing Jeremiah. Turns out Oliver was convinced that Jeremiah loved him as well and that the reason why Jeremiah never left David's mom was because of Larry."

"Do you believe that?" I asked softly, wondering how someone in love could listen to someone over their heart.

"No." He shook his head. "My dad didn't love him. My dad didn't love anyone but himself and the power he had over everyone."

"That's sad, but do you really think that?"

"It is sad and I don't just think that, I know." He sighed, and he clasped my hands tightly.

"How do you know?" I asked softly, my heart slowing as I stared at the adoration in his eyes.

"I know because there is nothing in heaven or hell that could stop me from loving and being with you. I'd move mountains, swim in oceans, jump in volcanoes, walk across hot coals, swing from trees in the Amazon to be with you. There is nothing and no one that could stop me. I'd visit the depths of the earth and sing to every angel of the sky to help find you if you ever got lost."

"You're just saying that," I said breathlessly.

"I would never just say that."

"I love you, Jakob."

"I love you too," he said, and leaned over and gave me a quick kiss. "And Penny loved her brother like nothing on earth. She plotted and planned for years, just waiting for the opportunity to take Larry down."

"I still can't believe it," I said, my mind blown. How I'd been fooled by her during that first meeting. I smiled to myself as a thought hit me. I wondered what Larry was thinking. He'd been totally bamboozled.

"I know." He laughed. "Turns out Penny knew exactly what she was talking about when she said people were listening that day you went to her house." He grinned. "She just forgot to tell you that it was her."

"Wow. And she's willing to come back from France and testify?"

"She's already back." He nodded. "Blake e-mailed her right before the ball. That's why he was late. They were e-mailing back and forth."

"I had no idea. I was wondering what he wasn't telling us, and now I guess I know why. He couldn't exactly tell us Steve was highly dangerous in front of Steve."

"Exactly." Jakob nodded. "But everything's okay now. We're going to be okay. We have the answers we needed. We can move on with our lives. Or at least try to." His hand moved to my ass, and I shifted.

"Jakob." I giggled. "Stop it."

"Stop what?" He licked his lips and then licked mine.

"I'm not making love to you in your hospital bed."

"Why not?" He grinned. "Just think how hot it would be."

"I'm not doing it." I shook my head. "No way, José. What if your stitches opened?"

"What if I told you it would make me feel better?"

"I'd say, oh well." I leaned forward and kissed him on the lips.

"Meanie." He made a face and then his eyes lit up. "There's something else I need to tell you."

I groaned as I looked at him. "I'm not sure how much more I can handle right now."

"The nurse came in when you were sleeping."

"Okay, and . . . ?"

"She asked me if you'd told me."

"Told you what?"

"About the baby." His eyes were alive with glee, and my heart stopped beating.

"What?"

"She asked if you'd told me about the baby. We're pregnant, Bianca." He brought my hands to his lips and kissed them hard. "We're having a baby."

"No way!" I shook my head in shock. "Are you sure?"

"As sure as I am that we're getting married just as soon as we make it out of the hospital."

"Oh, Jakob, I don't even know what to say."

"Just say yes, my darling. Just say yes."

fifteen

One Month Later

"There are two letters that have come for you, Bianca." Jakob held up a small yellow package and a flat white envelope as he walked into the bedroom.

"Who are they from?" I asked suspiciously as I sipped from a glass of cold water.

"Not sure," he said as he sat on the bed next to me. "Do you want me to open them for you first?"

"No." I shook my head and smiled at his worried expression adoringly. "I can check."

"I just don't want you to make yourself sick." He touched my forehead. "You're sure you're okay?"

"It's morning sickness, Jakob." I rolled my eyes. "Not the plague." I grabbed the letter and package from his hand. "I don't even need to be on bed rest."

"The doctor said you need to take care of yourself."

"That's just prenatal care, darling." I gave him a quick kiss on the lips, my heart thudding as I recognized Rosie's handwriting on the envelope. "All pregnant women have to take care of themselves."

"Well, you need to take extra special care."

"I guess that means there will be no secret excursions to any stranded islands." I laughed and stroked his face. "No hot sex in the sand as we wait for a boat to find us."

"Haha." He laughed and grabbed my hand and kissed it. "Who knew that would become your new fantasy? I wish I'd played it up for you more while we were there."

"I didn't really know you then." I laughed. "I would have slapped you and ran away and hid in the jungle. And most probably I'd have been eaten by a monkey."

"Or a boar," he said matter-of-factly, and I slapped him on the arm.

"I think this letter is from Rosie." I licked my lips nervously as I looked down.

"You sure you want to read it?" he questioned me, his eyes darkening at the sound of her name.

"Yeah." I nodded. "I want to know why she's writing."

"I don't want you to feel sorry for her." He looked angry. "She knew what she was doing. She knew that her father was evil incarnate. And she went along with his plan."

"But she was doing it for him," I said softly, my heart breaking all over again as I thought about my previous best friend. The one person I'd always thought had had my back. To know that it had all been a lie, well, it killed me.

"She knew better than to just go along with it," he said with a frown. "She wasn't some little kid being led astray."

"People do weird stuff for love," I said, and sighed. "She just wanted her dad to be there for her."

"I'm sorry, but I have no sympathy. She put your life in danger."

"Jakob," I said softly, and leaned back against the head-board. "I'm going to open the letter now."

"Read it aloud then," he said, and got up on the bed properly. "Tell me what she said."

"Fine," I said, and opened the letter slowly. It was on a single piece of lined paper, and I unfolded it. " 'Bianca, no matter what I say now, you will never believe me. I've lied to you more times than I can count. You have no reason to trust or believe me now. I'm not writing to you for your forgive-ness. I don't expect that. I'm writing to you because I truly am sorry. One day, you might believe me. But for now, accept this gift. Your friend, Rosie.' " My voice caught as I stopped reading. I looked back at the words, and I wasn't sure what to say.

"What gift?" Jakob said, frowning.

"I don't know." I shrugged and then sighed. "I wish I didn't feel so sad."

"Don't." Jakob's voice was unforgiving. "Her words are empty, meaningless." His voice was angry. "She still hasn't given a real reason for anything that happened."

"Maybe she doesn't know how to voice it?" I shrugged and sighed. I then looked at the small package and opened it quickly, wondering who this was from. There was a small green velvet box and an envelope. My breath caught as I stared at the handwriting on the envelope. It was my father's. Immediately, I felt tears in my eyes, and my chest grew heavy.

"Bianca, what's wrong?" Jakob's tone was sharp and concerned. "Is it the baby?"

"No." I shook my head and gulped. "My dad." I pursed my lips, and my heart exploded with love as Jakob brushed the tears away from my cheek and then kissed me softly. "This must be the gift Rosie is talking about. She found a way to get me this letter from my dad."

"Don't cry," he said. "Do you want to read it now?"

"Yes," I said, and opened the envelope carefully, not wanting to damage the letter inside. I pulled out the letter, and my heart banged at the familiar handwriting. "You read it," I said as I handed him the letter. "Please."

"Of course." He nodded and cleared his throat. He took the letter from me and started reading. "'My darling Bianca. If you're reading this, everything didn't go according to plan. I tried so hard for you, my dear, my darling daughter. I know that you most probably don't understand why I faked my death. I'm not sure I could understand myself if it wasn't in my head. My darling daughter, you were my life, my breath, my heart. Your mother and I were so thankful for every day we had with you. When you were born, your mother, selfless angel that she was, made me promise that everything that we both did in this world would be to protect you and to love you. And when she died, I failed you. I became a shell of myself. I blamed myself for so many things. I lived in the past, and I lived to regret it. I regretted it because you were still there with me, living, loving, breathing, and I squandered so many years. When I realized what had happened with Jeremiah and Oliver, when I realized that Larry was as evil and as cruel as I'd always imagined him to be, I knew I had to do something. They were coming for me. They were coming for you. And you, my beautiful, wonderful daughter, needed to be protected at all costs. I entered into a deal with the devil. I knew that Steve was unstable. I knew that I was taking a risk. That I might not make it. That my life as I knew it, my freedom, my sanctuary would be gone. But I willingly gave that up for you, my love. I gave it up because I would give ten thousand lives to save you. This letter means that I tried my hardest and something happened. Do not hate me or mourn me. Live your life. Love your life and be free. Free to do as you want. Free to love who you want. Free to think what you want. Never be afraid to speak up for what's right. Never be afraid to spread your wings and fly. Jump into the ocean and swim with the sharks. Your mother and I will both be watching over you. I know you may never understand the why or the how. I know you may never fully understand. But please forgive me and love me. I did it to protect you. I did it because it was the only solution I thought I had. My death for your life. Something had to give. Something and someone had to take Larry down. I would do it again. Just for you.

I did it all for you. For I will always love you. Your loving papa.'" Jakob's voice was soft as he finished reading the letter, and he held me in his arms as I sobbed.

"I hate him and I love him," I said as I cried, and Jakob's hands rubbed the back of my shirt and my hair softly. "Why couldn't he have told me what was going on?"

"He wanted to protect you, Bianca," Jakob whispered next to my ear. "He thought it was his best bet."

"I guess," I said, and opened the green velvet box to see what was inside. "What's this?" I said, and looked at a small silver ring. I looked up at Jakob and he shrugged. I pulled the ring out slowly and stared at it. I'd never seen it before and was puzzled why my father had sent it to me. I looked the ring over and then noticed a small indent where the ring had been marked. I started crying when I read what it said: *Nick and Angelina forever.* I showed Jakob the ring and he smiled at me tenderly.

"They're both in heaven now looking down at you," he said as he held me close to him. "They are your protectors in heaven, and I'm your protector on earth."

"I love you, Jakob Bradley," I said as I gazed into his strong blue eyes. "I love you more than you'll ever know."

"And I love you too," he said, and kissed the side of my face. "Jakob and Bianca, forever and ever," he whispered into my ear. "Nothing will ever split us apart."

epilogue

Two Years Later

The hot sun beating down on my face was oddly comforting. I lazily opened one eye and sat up slightly to check up on Isabella and Jakob. A wide smile covered my face as I watched Jakob patiently building a sand castle with her. Isabella was her daddy's mini-me, with her bright blue eyes. She beamed up at him as her little hands crashed down on the turret that had taken Jakob an hour to create.

"All falls down, Daddy!" She giggled as her fingers played in the sand.

"Yes, all down," Jakob said, smiling at her adoringly. He leaned over and kissed her cheek.

"Daddy, slobber." Isabella giggled again and then jumped up and ran over to me, her chubby little legs moving as quickly as they could. "Mummy, Daddy, slobber." She fell down next to me, and I pulled her into my arms.

"Only because he loves you." I kissed the top of her head, and Jakob walked over to us with a huge smile on his face.

"Daddy loves me, and Daddy loves Mommy," Isabella said as she pulled away from me. "And Daddy loves baby Mickey." She reached down and rubbed my belly.

"We're not calling him Mickey, Isabella." I laughed, and Jakob and I gazed into each other's eyes.

"Yes, Mickey," she said with a small pout, and then looked up at Jakob. "Daddy, please?"

"How can I say no to that face?" he asked me with a smile as he sat and put his arm around me.

"You'll have to learn to soon." I smiled and leaned back into him. We gazed out at the aquamarine ocean, both of us silent as we sat there with Isabella lying comfortably in my arms.

"What are you thinking about?" he asked me softly, his fingers twining in my hair.

"That first night on the island with you," I said, and looked at him. "How dangerous and magical it felt and how confused I was by my attraction to you."

"Do you wish I'd taken you there instead of here?"

"No, Miami Beach is fine." I looked to the right and stared at the bright red lifeguard hut and the sunbathers a couple of yards beyond it. "I'm not sure I would have wanted to have gone back there with Izzy." I reached over and touched his arm. "It's still raw, and as glad as I am to have the whole truth finally come out, it still makes me feel uncomfortable at times to relive the memories."

"I understand." He nodded, and his eyes searched mine. "You feel safe now though?"

"Yes, I feel safe and loved and at peace." I sighed in contentment. "This is the life I've always wanted."

"You don't regret not still writing your scintillating movie reviews?" He laughed as I made a face at him.

"I don't miss writing them, and I'm sure no one misses reading them." I giggled, and Jakob's eyes searched mine.

"I miss reading them," he said with a small smile. "I miss trying to guess what you really thought about the movie."

"I still can't believe you used to read them." I shook my head. "It boggles me that you were actually attracted to me before we even met."

"I guess some part of me has always known that you were the one for me. Maybe it was our destiny to be together."

"You don't believe in destiny." I rolled my eyes at him and gasped as I felt the baby kicking. I grabbed his hand and placed it on my stomach. "He's kicking again," I said as I lay back and Jakob rubbed my stomach.

"Mickey kicking?" Isabella started talking animatedly, and I gave Jakob a look.

"Darling, your brother's name is going to be Nicholas, not Mickey," he said, and looked at me. I nodded, my throat suddenly constricted with emotion.

"Like Granddad?" Isabella asked, and I nodded, my heart overflowing with love and happiness toward my family.

"Yes, just like Granddad."

"Okay," she said, and jumped up. "Daddy, I wanna build a sand castle."

"Another one?" He groaned, and I laughed.

"Yes, Daddy." She smiled happily and tugged on his hand. "Come and help me."

"Fine." He jumped up and looked down at me. "Are you sure you want to go back to get your PhD? I'm more than happy for you to be a housewife."

"You wish." I smiled at him. "Besides, I'm only going to school part-time, and I'm going to be assisting one of Blake's classes."

"It's a good thing I trust you," Jakob said lightly as he stared down at me.

"Or what?"

"Or maybe I wouldn't be so understanding that your best friend is a man."

"You're my best friend, Jakob."

"Well, your other best friend, then."

I laughed as he made a face at me. "You have known that Blake and I are only friends forever, honey. You can't still be jealous."

"I'll always be jealous of the other men in your life." He knelt down next to me. "But I know you love me, and I know you're mine. You'll always be mine, and I'll always love you. You've made me happier than I ever imagined I'd be. I love you even more each day, and I will never stop loving you or wanting you. You've blessed me with the most wonderful family. I'm so grateful that we're one big happy family. Almost like the von Trapps."

"Oh, Jakob." I laughed and held his face carefully as I kissed him. "I love you more than words can say. I'll never stop loving you. And we're nothing like the von Trapps. We're not fleeing the Nazis, and I'm not a nun."

"You can dress up as a nun tonight, if you want." He grinned, his hand sliding down my waist. "That would make it a very interesting night."

"You wish, honey," I said with a giggle. "You wish." He laughed as he stood up and walked over to Isabella.

I leaned back and let my face soak in the sun's rays as I thought about the outfit I'd wear to bed tonight so that we could role-play one of his fantasies. I smiled to myself, secure in the knowledge that all of my dreams had finally come true.